"What a provocative idea! I found the novel fascinating ... an intriguing story. It bears (no pun intended) not only further reading, but further investigation. A cautionary note: Don't have anyone read this book to President George Bush and Homeland Security. It might give them terrible ideas."

ED ASNER, ACTOR

When his friends became drunk he would often shut them up, and suddenly during the night let in his lions, leopards and bears all of them harmless so that his friends on awakening at dawn, or worse, during the night, would find lions and leopards and bears in the room with themselves; and some even died from this cause....

The Life of Antonius Heliogabalus, Aelius Lampridius, XXVI, trans. David Magie, Loeb Classical Library, 1924

No one knows how the ancients trained the great beasts; and we know nothing of how animals were domesticated. But according to the ancients, quiet "gentling" methods were used, including, in Egypt at least, music. The methods for training and conditioning the wild animals have been either lost or forgotten over the centuries, except as they may have been revived by an occasional genius.

***Circus! From Rome to Ringling*, Marian Murray, Appleton Century-Crofts, Inc., New York, 1956**

There are not a great many wild animals in Egypt, in spite of the fact that it borders on Libya. Such as there are both wild and tame are without exception held to be sacred.... Bears...are buried wherever they happen to be found lying dead.

***The Histories*, II, 65-67, Herodotus**

It seems clear that these exotic marvels were brought to Egypt for their curiosity value. Whether any of them were "performing" bears, we have not the slightest hint. They are attested as trained entertainers in Egypt only during the Roman Period, as evidenced by a charming bronze statuette of a dancing bear, now in the collections of the Brooklyn Museum.

***The Animal World of the Pharaohs*, Ch. 8: "The Royal Menagerie," pp 195-197, Patrick F. Houlihan, Thames and Hudson Ltd., London, 1996.**

"And someone has been sleeping in my bed!" the little bear squeaked in his Tiny Little Voice. "AND HERE SHE IS!"
Goldilocks and The Three Bears.

I fear we shall outsleep the coming *morn*
As much as we this night have overwatched!
A Midsummer Night's Dream
William Shakespeare

Would *Le Gros* Serpent have been heard by the ears of one he wished to be deaf? Does the white chief burn his powder in the faces of his brothers? Does he ever miss his aim, when seriously bent to kill? returned Duncan, smiling with well acted sincerity....Magua muttered a few words, inaudibly, between his teeth, before he continued, aloud: Can the Delawares swim, too, as well as crawl in the bushes? Where is *Le Gros* Serpent? Duncan, who perceived by the use of these Canadian appellations, that his late companions were much better known to his enemies than himself, answered, reluctantly: He also is gone down with the water.
The Last of the Mohicans
James Fenimore Cooper

Cape Chidley
N
Labrador Sea
Mer du Labrador
CANADA
Nain
Davis Inlet
Hopedale
Makkovik
Postville
QUEBEC / QUEBEC
TERRE-NEUVE
NEWFOUNDLAND
Smallwood Reservoir
Rigolet
North West River
Cartwright
Labrador City
Wabush
Churchill Falls
Fl Churchill R
Happy Valley-Goose Bay
Port Hope Simpson
Str of Belle Isle / Dét de Belle Isle
Forteau
St Anthony
QUEBEC / QUÉBEC
Roddickton
Port au Choix
Gulf of Saint-Lawrence
Golfe du Saint-Laurent
Baie Verte
Fogo
Rocky Harbour
Twillingate
LEGEND / LÉGENDE
Provincial capital / Capitale provinciale
Other populated places / Autres lieux habités
Trans-Canada Highway / La Transcanadienne
Major road / Route principale
Ferry route / Traversier
International boundary / Frontière internationale
Provincial boundary / Limite provinciale
Deer Lake
Bishop's Falls
Lewisporte
Gander
ATLANTIC OCEAN
OCEAN ATLANTIQUE
Corner Brook
Stephenville
Buchans
Grand Falls-Windsor
Bonavista
Glovertown
St George's
Clarenville
Carbonear
St Alban's
Bay Roberts
St John's
Channel-Port aux Basques
Burgeo
Harbour Breton
Placentia
Holyrood
Ferryland
Cabot Strait
Détroit de Cabot
Marystown
Burin
Trepassey
Grand Bank
Cape Race
Saint-Pierre et Miquelon
FRANCE
The Grand Banks of Newfoundland
Les Grands Bancs de Terre-Neuve
Scale / Échelle
100 0 100 200 300
km km
© 2000. Her Majesty the Queen in Right of Canada, Natural Resources Canada.
Sa Majesté la Reine du chef du Canada, Ressources naturelles Canada.

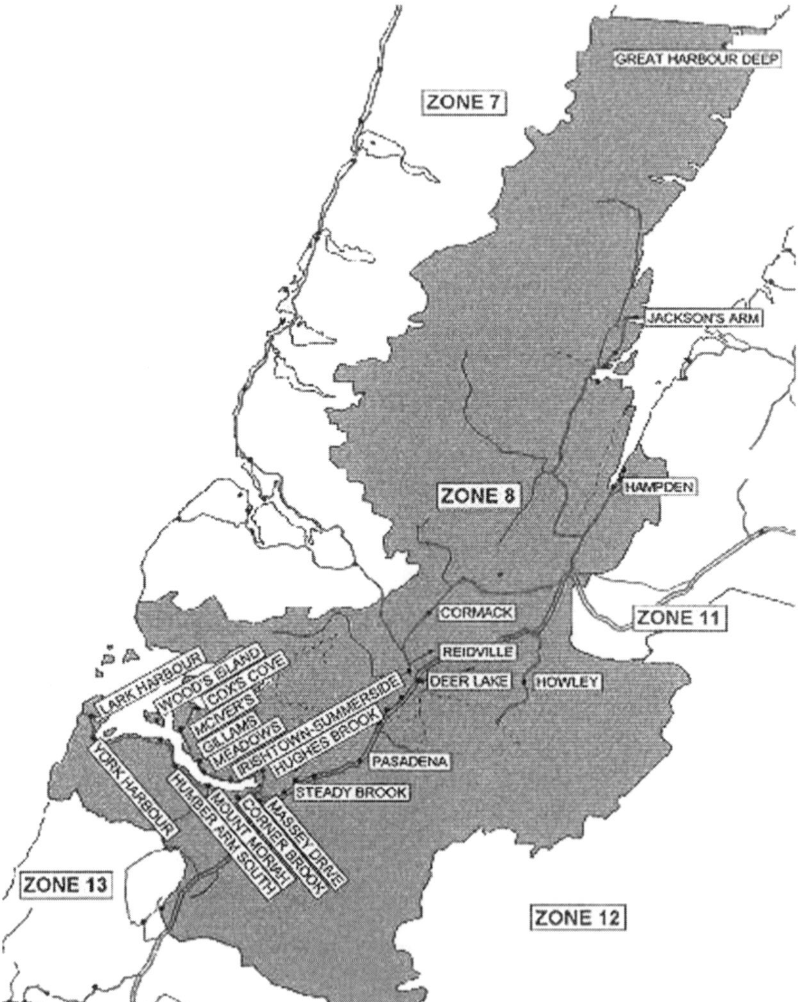
GREAT HARBOUR DEEP
ZONE 7
JACKSON'S ARM
ZONE 8
HAMPDEN
CORMACK
ZONE 11
REIDVILLE
DEER LAKE
HOWLEY
LARK HARBOUR
WOOD'S ISLAND
COX'S COVE
MCIVER'S
GILLAMS
MEADOWS
IRISHTOWN-SUMMERSIDE
HUGHES BROOK
PASADENA
STEADY BROOK
YORK HARBOUR
HUMBER ARM SOUTH
MOUNT MORIAH
CORNER BROOK
MASSEY DRIVE
ZONE 13
ZONE 12

WALTER MALLERY

GROS MORNE JUSTICE

A NOVEL

FLANKER PRESS LTD.
ST. JOHN'S, NL
2004

National Library of Canada Cataloguing in Publication

Mallery, Walter, 1952-
Gros Morne justice / Walter Mallery.

ISBN 1-894463-65-X

I. Title.

PS8626.A45G76 2004 C813'.6 C2004-901757-8

This is a work of fiction. Names, characters, places, and incidents are either the imaginary creations of the author, or they are used fictionally, and any resemblance to actual persons, living or dead, except for public personalities, actual historical events, or geographically identified locales, is wholly coincidental.

Cover photo © Kevin Redmond
Author photo credit: Carl Senna

PRINTED IN CANADA

First printing June 2004
Second printing September 2004

FLANKER PRESS LTD.
P.O. BOX 2522, STATION C
ST. JOHN'S, NL CANADA A1C 6K1
TOLL FREE: 1-866-739-4420 TELEPHONE: (709) 739-4477 FAX: (709) 739-4420
WWW.FLANKERPRESS.COM

Canada

We acknowledge the financial support of the Government of Canada through the Book Publishing Industry Development Program (BPIDP) for our publishing program.

CONTENTS

Acknowledgements

To my wife Bet, who has helped make my tale and dream of Gros Morne Justice come true. She was the one who let me know it was worth the challenge.

To Carl Senna, my editor, who spent long hours of the day and night to complete this novel, with whom I have shared many laughs. His professionalism I truly admire.

To the team at Flanker Press, who (I have learned in a short time) will stop at nothing and do their very best. A special thanks also to Paul Butler. What a great, honest and hardworking team.

I want to thank them all for believing in my novel, for I could not have done it without their help.

I just told a story, my biggest lie ever.

Glossary

Alders: thick plant bushes found in Newfoundland

Boar: male bear

Cremains: cremated human remains

Honey Burn: scent bait of honey burned over sterno can to attract bears

Fjord: Viking word for lake

Grilse: young salmon, a salmon that fishermen and fisherwomen may legally keep

Panhandler: a bear that begs for food

Scat: bear dung

Sow: female bear

Sterno can: container of solid fuel

Tuckamore: thicket of trees bent horizontal by fierce winds, under which bears hide, make trails, and escape detection; the horizontal tree growth gives meaning to the local expression, "to walk on the tops of pines"

For my daughter, Krista

Prologue

Newfoundland, an island in the North Atlantic

Newfoundland, as viewed on a map, is an island in the North Atlantic Ocean, a clump of earth facing the Gulf of St. Lawrence and Labrador. The island is a hard place to make a living, as you might imagine, for at this latitude and longitude the planet is less fertile and less welcoming to plant and animal life beyond a brief summer. The people of Newfoundland are generous, hospitable and charming. The island's two main industries, fishing and logging, absorb most of the labour force and offer more lucrative employment to residents than farming. The land is a challenge to agriculture because of its extensive aridity, a short growing season and limited crop yield. But the scenery is beautiful beyond compare. A few remote, northern mountain slopes hidden from the direct sun have snow year-round, providing a picturesque vista suggestive of an alpine landscape. When the snow melts away completely on the mountains, they offer hikers and campers virgin flatlands and forests of aspen, birch and conifers. The island lakes and rivers, abundant with trout, salmon and other fish, run so clear and so clean in the warm months that you can drink the water from them. The rivers and ocean are the darkest blues you will ever see.

The island has five months of hard winter with lots of snow, so it may not be the place for those less actively inclined or those seeking temperate climes for rest and relaxation. On the other hand, the residents socialize more in the cold months than they do in the summer. As you may imagine, many of them live off their savings from work in the other seven months. Among the islanders you find an unusually strong communal spirit. With less to do in the winter, they often throw parties, snowmobile, ski, improve themselves through education and craft and travel for work elsewhere in Canada. Some of them inevitably get into mischief.

Caribou and moose are plentiful; the island, moreover, boasts thousands of black bears. Indeed, there are almost as many bears as there are human families on the island, but the two seldom meet, for the meeting is rarely welcomed by the bear unless the bear has learned to beg for food near tourist spots or homes. Newfoundland is a must place to visit if you are a nature lover, a sport fisherman or a hunter.

Not long ago the bears in and around the great national park Gros Morne and the town of Deer Lake turned against the residents for reasons that are still mostly a matter of speculation, but no doubt those reasons are closely associated with man's folly.

DEER LAKE, A TOWN NEAR GROS MORNE NATIONAL PARK

Deer Lake attracts tourists all year round. The town, set in the richest farmland of the region, has a lake that extends twenty-five miles south toward the larger community of Corner Brook. One of the reasons for the popularity of the town of Deer Lake, however, is Gros Morne National Park, a UNESCO World

Heritage Site, twenty miles to the north, with 5,225 square miles of hiking trails, wildlife and wilderness. The immense park has a mountain range straddling the coast and forming what some would describe as the Eastern Rockies. Our story begins the first Sunday afternoon in May, when many of the residents of Deer Lake are busy cleaning yards, painting fences and preparing for a full evening of social life.

PART I

1

The Bear Hunters

Jack Crandall was on the pathway leading into his ranch-style lodge, an attractive property so well kept that Martha Stewart herself would have been proud to display its exterior view in her magazine. In the front porch, there were petunias, azaleas, violets and other seasonal flowers transferred from the greenhouse. The lodge was nestled before a hill of spruce, alders and birch, trimmed and arranged behind a well-manicured lawn meadow. The lodge was much larger than the Crandalls needed, so the extra space was converted into bedrooms for visiting hunters.

On one side of the house was a bountiful vegetable garden a hundred feet in length. Near it was a rustic old barn Jack used for storage. The walls of the outbuilding were weathered and grey and stood fifteen feet to the gable's peak, the same as its width. Inside hung mechanical equipment for snowmobiles, skis and sleds, all-terrain vehicles, and bikes. Sitting on shelves along the length of the barn were axes and saws, shovels and ladders, motors, fishing rods and other gear used in the outfitting business.

Inside the house, a woman, her brown hair flecked with strands of grey, stood in the kitchen with a telephone to her ear.

The person calling asked to speak to Jack, her husband, or their son, Calvin.

"Calvin's not here just now," Dorothy Crandall answered. "Jack's finishing up work out back. I can take a message and have him call you back."

The caller was insistent. He needed to speak with Jack right away.

"I'll have to put you on hold and fetch him," she said. "It'll take only a few moments."

As she put the telephone down on the counter next to the sink, she turned to see that Jack had just entered the kitchen.

"It's Rick Preston," she said.

Jack took the receiver. "Yes, Rick. Tell the guys Calvin and I will be at the airport in an hour." He hung up the telephone. "Damned impatient, them Americans," he said to his wife. "You'd think I was guiding them to a movie about shooting bears and they had to be there at a certain time." He chuckled and shook his head.

"They just want to get going, Jack," Dorothy said.

"They don't understand bears, Dorothy," he responded.

Jack and Dorothy Crandall lived in the house with their son, Calvin. The young man was to accompany his father on an outfitting hunt for a party of six Americans organized by Long Island stockbroker Rick Preston. The Americans each had hopes of shooting a black bear trophy to take home. But Calvin would be delayed for the hunt. That spring he had found a job at a funeral home in Deer Lake, working for the new director who had taken it over the previous year. Calvin had not yet returned from work, so his father was considering what to do if he did not show up.

"I'll call him," said Dorothy.

"No," said Jack, "I'll be finished out back in fifteen minutes. He still has some time."

Dorothy Crandall, a gentle woman with a smooth face and brown eyes, was a few days younger than Jack. She was so devoted to her husband that she fretted over his delay in meeting with the hunters, knowing how hard he worked to develop his outfitting business. But she knew that he adored Calvin, and the boy, all of twenty years old, would have to mess up very seriously before his father would call him to task.

Jack and Dorothy had been high-school sweethearts in Corner Brook. Like so many others, they married after graduation. They started out renting a house in Deer Lake, but after a few years they were able to get a mortgage on the property they now owned—a lodge on four hundred acres, overlooking a small lake on a dead-end logging road. The lodge was about eight hundred yards off the main north-south highway. Jack and his son ran a very successful outfitting business there.

Before long, Calvin's shiny new Dodge Ram pulled into the driveway next to his mother's Pontiac. The truck was a gift from his father, yet another of the perks from the success of last year's outfitting.

The tall, dark-haired young man standing with Dorothy in the kitchen and greeting Jack had a dimple in his chin. He was a handsome youth, slightly taller and thinner than his father.

"So, Dad," he said. "We're on for tonight with the Americans."

"I see you're here at last," Jack said wearily. "It takes you all day to cremate somebody?"

"It wasn't just one body," said Calvin. "There's a lot to learn about cremations. Norm's got more bodies stacked up than you would believe, and he can't keep the ovens burning long enough."

"Pretty gruesome business, I'd say," joined Dorothy.

"It pays the bills. And it's a respectable profession. Somebody's got to do it."

"I dunno," said Jack. "I wouldn't do it unless I had to, that's for sure. I can take dead animals, but not dead folks. Gives me the creeps to see a dead person."

"It's all the same, Dad. Heck, we eat moose and caribou, and I tell you, animal steaks and human flesh look the same. Why, I bet we could cut down the cost of funerals immensely by just feeding dead people to bears and foxes."

"Oh, hush," said Dorothy. "What a thing to say, Calvin!"

"It's the truth. We're the same meat."

"You ready to help your dad on the hunt?" Dorothy asked, changing the subject.

"Eager," he said, "if the guests are."

"They sure are," said Jack.

"That's an advantage. And paid up?" Calvin asked.

"Paid in full."

"Americans," Calvin said.

Jack rolled his eyes.

"You fellows had better start moving," Dorothy said. "The hunters are waiting on you."

Dorothy watched the men leave. She worried about Jack and Calvin when they went outfitting a bear hunt. They were so excited about the fun and the money that she began to wonder if safety was really a priority. She was looking forward to a family trip to Big Falls for salmon fishing after this hunt was over. It would be nice, she thought, to know the men would be in one piece for the trip. A guide had been killed a few days earlier by a bear forty miles away, on the other side of Corner Brook. But Jack said they would be careful. After all, there was no way Jack would put Calvin in harm's way. And Jack had assured her a thousand times that he had lived and worked this area all his life and knew the woods like the back of his hand. He really loved the animals on the island, she thought. It occurred to her, not for the first time, either, that Jack had been teaching Calvin the ways of nature from the time he could walk and talk. The only time Jack seemed worried about Calvin, she noticed, was when the boy talked of one day opening a funeral home of his own. Calvin was unmoved by his father's protests.

"And if there aren't enough bears to hunt," Calvin would say, "what will we do? Wait for tourists to find Gros Morne? No way. I need a Plan B."

Plan B was obvious. More and more he was talking about the profits and excitement of going to school to learn the profession of embalming and cremating bodies.

Dorothy had to admit it did make sense. A funeral home could be insurance, but only if outfitting didn't work out. This was Calvin's fourth year helping his father in guiding. She glanced at the calendar on her kitchen wall, and the handwriting on it reminding her that she was going to be cooking meals for the next six weeks.

Her thoughts turned to their plans for the little enterprise. The men were thinking of expanding the outfitting side of the lodge. Jack and Dorothy would handle the summer tourist season for lodgers, and gradually Calvin would take over all of the hunting. Dorothy had seen the excitement in Calvin's face one evening after supper a few weeks earlier. Next year, he had told her, they would offer fishing, canoeing and rafting trips, along with the outfitting for hunters. What excited Dorothy most was the prospect of having Calvin working side by side with them the following year. What more could a family ask of their son? And who knew? He might even settle down with a girlfriend. Calvin seemed to have a different one each month. Perhaps, she sighed to herself, when the business was larger and more profitable he'd find someone to marry and give his mother some grandchildren to spoil. It would be disappointing, though, to see Calvin just up and leave the lodge and outfitting. Jack would be disappointed, after he had made plans to leave the company to Calvin. But already she began to fear that would most likely happen, probably when Calvin decided to start a family. Then he would want a steady income, probably from something like a funeral home—people have to die, and the dead have to be buried or cremated.

All Calvin talked about was the money Norm Cotten made from cremating and burying people, Norm's frequent trips to the States, how Norm wasn't much older than Calvin and already owned a Mercedes, a Ford Explorer, a BMW, a fifty-foot sailboat, and a house and condo in St. John's. Norm was even talking, Calvin said once, of buying his own Lear Jet. How could a funeral home make so much money in Newfoundland? That's the national health insurance for you, she harrumphed to herself. She resented Norm Cotten for putting such outlandish ideas in her Calvin's head, filling him with dreams of the money he could make, boasts that could not possibly be altogether true.

While Dorothy mused in her kitchen, Jack and Calvin were at the airport in Deer Lake with the American hunters. The Crandalls were sitting at a table, drinking coffee and talking about the prospects for their family outfitting business. They called it "Jack's Outfitting." The six sportsmen, all on their first hunt in Newfoundland, met their hosts after they claimed their luggage and picked up last-minute reading material at the gift shop next to the cafeteria.

On the road to the lodge, the men shared the two Crandall trucks, loaded down with their gear. Suddenly, Jack pointed to a large black bear they were passing on the opposite side of the road. Both trucks pulled over to look at the bear, which was not amused by the attention. It turned around and disappeared with a *whoosh* into the alders.

At the lodge, Dorothy served the men a large roast of moose meat with all the trimmings. Some of them had never eaten moose meat and they were very impressed.

"Has a beef taste," one of them remarked, and the others agreed.

After the meal, Jack began telling stories of hunting and fishing in the area, and of people being mauled by bears. Soon the beer flowed freely. Jack advised the Americans to be cautious of the Newfoundland black bear, not to try to outrun them because the bears had been clocked at forty-five miles an hour; moreover, he said, unlike the mainland black bear, these were larger, more aggressive animals, more carnivorous and less intimidated by people they encountered. When it was time for the men to call it an evening, Jack told them that they would start hunting in mid-afternoon and they would stay out until dark.

"Get a good sleep, and stay alert tomorrow."

"Bring on Old Smokey," Rick replied, standing up and walking unsteadily to the bathroom. Jack hoped Preston would be sober by the next evening. A client showing up drunk on the day of the hunt meant the expedition would not go ahead.

As they went to bed, Dorothy told Jack she was concerned about the drinking and the fact that not one of the men had hunted bear before. Jack kissed her and said, "They will have big heads in the morning, but they will be fine by the afternoon."

The next morning a rifle shot rang through the hills and brought all the lodge guests outside. There in a clearing near the woods, one of the hunting party, Ted Schultz, a heavy-set taxidermist, was testing his .30-06 rifle. The weapon was smoking; he had fired at a bull's eye tacked to a tree, striking the outer circle of the target. He turned to the other hunters boasting, "Beat that shot, boys."

"Where's my blindfold!" Rick quipped.

Schultz turned to Dorothy. "When's breakfast?"

"Well, it sure won't take long to cook up that target," she said, "but what would the others like for breakfast?"

"Nothing for me," said Rick. "I'm going back to bed for a while."

But the others were hungry. "Sausage and eggs would be great, Dorothy," one of them said.

Two hours later, Rick rolled out of bed and sat down to left-over sausages in the kitchen.

"Say, Jack," he asked, holding one up. "How about baiting the bears with this sausage?"

"Nope," said Jack. "Bears have finicky tastes. They don't like garlic and pepper in their meat."

Jack explained to them that he had once tried sausage on bears and found that it never worked at bait sites.

"You should rub yourselves with garlic and pepper," he said. "If a bear starts to bite you, it will be turned off by the seasoning, I assure you."

Jack went through a list of things he wanted them to bring along on the hunt. All the gear, he said, had to fit into a single backpack. Hunting black bears required sitting and waiting. Most of all, a hunter had to be prepared to move and shoot as quickly as possible when the moment came, which was usually when least expected. Then there was the deadly possibility of the black bear ambushing the stalker. In the woods, he said, all the natural advantages of the forest are with a critter that can smell hunters hundreds of yards away, and with keen ears, bears can detect faraway sounds that a human could not. They can even sense the size and weight of a hiker from the vibrations of his foot treads. Hunting bears in Newfoundland was not a sport for the novice without a seasoned guide. A greenhorn in the forest looking for a small 150-pound bear, much less an 800-pound boar, would be suicidal.

"Take your practice shots and be ready to commence by three o'clock," Jack said. "Calvin and I will pick you up then, and we will be hunting until dark. In the meantime, we'll be in town getting doughnuts, grease and butcher scraps for bait."

"And, guys," Calvin said. "Remember, no booze or anything else like that."

"You mean smokes," Rick said.

"No, he means marijuana," said Jack.

The six men made a garrulous lot. They were full of excitement, swapping lies and rumours of bear attacks, wounded bears and other strange bear anecdotes of Newfoundland. Jack had learned from Schultz that three of the group worked together on Long Island building houses, and for years they had discussed bear hunting. Schultz intended to mount their trophies. The three were in their early thirties: Besides Shultz, there was Rick Preston, an independent Wall Street broker, married with two girls. The third was Don Beckman, a divorced bottling plant manager living with his new girlfriend for about three months. He had joked over supper that she wanted hunting banned. "If she wants me," he said, "then the hunting comes with me."

That afternoon, when Jack and Calvin returned to fetch them, the Americans were outdoors in front of the lodge, ready to hunt.

"Shoot only single mature bears that are taller and wider than a forty-five-gallon bait barrel," explained Jack. "No cubs. It's illegal to shoot a sow with a cub. This is good for bear management and for safety reasons. If you should accidentally shoot a cub, the sow will be really upset and dangerous, so for God's sake, be careful."

Calvin, Rick, Schultz and Don made up one team. Jack guided the rest.

It was a good time to hunt. It had been several seasons since Jack had seen so many bears in a single evening. His outfit saw fourteen bears in the area, and they took five, including one at 400 pounds. Jack had also seen a sow with cubs and two smaller bears at a clearing in the distance.

"These are trophies of a lifetime," he said to the men. "The head sizes are all record book class. All in one evening!"

Meanwhile, in Calvin's group, everyone but Rick had taken a bear, and he was not too happy about it. He complained of Calvin's choice of bait site. Schultz told Rick to calm down. This made him even angrier, and again he went after Calvin, asking him to switch sites for tomorrow. At the end of the first night, Rick was in a dark mood. It had not improved by morning, when the others posed outside the lodge taking photos of their prize bears, laughing, bragging and fooling around while Jack and Calvin skinned out the bears and cut up the meat for transport back to the States.

Rick had not gotten up for breakfast or lunch, so Calvin went to his room to check on him. When he returned, he pulled Jack aside to whisper in the kitchen.

"Rick seems a little under the weather."

"He's disappointed," said Jack. "How would you feel spending all that money to come this far, only to go home empty-handed, especially when everyone else has one?"

"There are no guarantees," Calvin said. "Anyway, yesterday was just the first day."

"That's right," said Jack. "A good outfitter can always make a succesful hunt."

On the third day, Rick, red-eyed and unkempt, was still bearless, but he seemed resigned.

"Sorry about my temper," he said to Calvin.

"That's okay. No drinking still, right?"

"Gotcha."

Calvin left Rick at a new stand and went on. Almost an hour later, he heard a shot from Rick's site. In the thirty minutes that it took him to reach the stand, he heard a second shot. When he arrived, he found a very excited Rick.

"I shot a bear!"

"Good, Rick. Where is it?"

"I don't know," he said. "It must have run away. I know I hit the sucker. Man, it was a good size."

Beyond the clearing, next to the scent bait, Calvin found a two-and-a-half-year-old boar, shot through the chest. At last, even Rick had a bear to mount.

At the camp that night, the hunters thanked the Crandall's for a great hunt.

"It's a nice bear," said Calvin. "A little on the small side, but a keeper."

"You'll get a bigger one next time, Rick," Jack assured the American.

"You think so, huh?" Rick said. Despite the size of his kill, he was in much better spirits.

The next afternoon, while Dorothy was preparing the bunks for another hunting party arriving on the weekend, Jack and Calvin were baiting—Jack in the Big Falls area and Calvin near the park a few miles away. When Jack returned to the lodge, he waited for

Calvin on his screen porch in the dark. The minutes passed swiftly as he watched for the Dodge Ram's headlights to turn into the drive.

It had always been Jack's hope to raise a son free of the hardships he had endured early in his life, one of abandonment and sorrow. Over the years, he had often heard the gruff voice that haunted him since childhood.

Don't you show any tears. Don't you cry out.

And he could feel the slap of the belt on his back, again and again, as he fought back the tears and the urge to scream.

Stop. Please stop.

But the belt would fall again and again, and fall yet again, upon his back and arms and legs, leaving cruel welts and bleeding sores.

Soon Jack would cry out loud, only to fall silent as the brutish male voice said once more, *Didn't I tell you not to say a word? Can't you take it like a man? Be a man, boy. Take it. Now, for that you're going to get twenty more licks.*

Months later he had learned that accepting the lashes made it easier and quicker when the man gave him his "Saturday night licks." It only hurt a little while, he learned when he was eight. If he just stood there, loose and limber, the blows hurt only up to five smacks and then the pain began to recede, the nerves under his skin numb from the repeated whipping. By the twentieth, he felt merely a release from pain.

But he wanted all the more to kill his stepfather. How he hated him!

In one sense he had done him a favour, Jack thought many years later, by making him inured to the blows that caused other boys to cry and to submit in fistfights. Accustomed to being hit, Jack was a tough fighter, and none of the older boys at school wanted to tangle with him.

His capacity for pain not only earned him respect, but he fancied once becoming a prizefighter, having read in a newspaper that boxers were trained to take punches without flinching or stopping from counterpunching their opponent. There had been two photographs of boxing champions Yvon Durelle and Rocky Marciano, both of whom could give as good as they took in the ring, and, the caption had read, "gave heavier punches the more they were punched."

Yes, he could take pain, could control his feelings. But the one thing he had never controlled was his temper, his fits of rage. Though Jack had never killed a man, he had taught quite a few a lesson they never forgot.

Jack sighed. Calvin was over an hour late, so he decided to drive over to the park area.

The first thing he noticed when he reached the bait site where Rick had first hunted was Calvin's truck, empty but idling. There was something about the empty truck in the darkness that made Jack feel uneasy.

He took his 12-gauge semi-automatic out of its case and loaded it, a Remington that he had owned for over ten years. He had bought it from a hunter with his outfit. It was not registered, and he figured he never would register the shotgun; the new federal gun registry was, at least in his mind, a waste of time and money. He turned off Calvin's ignition and lights. As he listened beside the truck, Jack heard a familiar, dreaded noise. It was the sound of a bear clawing and snapping its teeth, a sound that Jack knew well not to ignore. The animal was warning him to stay away. He fired a warning shot, but instead of hearing the bear running away, he heard faint brush movements. The sound told him that the animal, being an ambush hunter, was stalking him and waiting for him to move to a place ideal for surprise attack.

"Calvin," Jack called. "Calvin, you out there?"

He knew now that there was no sense trying to hide from the bear. It was already positioned to blindside him.

Jack called his son a few more times, but there was no response. Taking a flashlight from Calvin's truck, he guided himself down the path into the thicket of alders and pine, following the bear's sound, stepping slowly and quietly until he heard again the loud *click-click* and snapping of teeth. He shone his light toward the sound, which seemed to be coming from a spot some twenty yards from the bait site. There Jack spotted Calvin's bait pails tipped on their sides. A few feet ahead of the buckets, on the ground, a dark red stain glistened in the flashlight's glow.

Jack saw wet blood smeared on the bark of nearby trees. A few yards up the path, he spotted something. Turning to the side of the trail and standing at an angle, he discerned that the pathway had been cleared by a large animal. The fir trees made it difficult for him to identify it. He pushed his way through the thick boughs, stepping on something soft that gave way under his weight. Not knowing whether it was alive or not, he jumped, frightened. Regaining his composure, he focused the flashlight beam on the spot.

It was Calvin.

His son was lying face down, and in the flashlight beam, the body showed fatal mauling. Jack rolled him over and saw that one side of Calvin's face was deeply clawed and bloody, and where his eyes had been were now dark and empty holes of black horror. The lower part of his body was mutilated from savage tears to the stomach and upper thighs.

His son was gone. Right then and there he wanted to guarantee that the bear that had killed his son would never attack another human being. He felt tears in his eyes, but they were not the tears of grief. They were the tears of a man so angry he could barely see anything. He was seized with the desire to kill someone or something, and the bout lasted for several moments, as he groped aimlessly about the clearing.

Within seconds, there came a warning of possession. The bear that had killed his son was claiming exclusive rights to its meal.

"Woof."

Suddenly, the bear charged him from the right side of a dark clump of alder, closing in on him in a fraction of a second with one whooshing black motion. There was just enough time for Jack to point the 12-gauge's muzzle at the sound and fire, pumping and firing again and again at the black shadow until he heard nothing more but the echo retreating through the blue-grey smoke. When the air cleared, he took the flashlight and inspected the claw prints of the bear. By the size of them, he estimated the bear to be well over two hundred pounds.

But now with an empty weapon, Jack knew he should hurry back to his truck. It was too dangerous to remain at the site. It was unlikely that the bear would soon be back to chance more hot lead, unless it was very hungry or had a cub around the area. There was nothing more he could do for Calvin but take him out of the woods.

It took him a few minutes to get the body back to the truck. He laid his son on the ground near the side of the pathway, and for a moment closed his eyes, trying to compose himself and regain his breath. It was a close call, he thought. *Damned bear! I hope I killed that bitch!*

Then the bear reappeared.

Fearing for his life, Jack left Calvin's body and jumped in the truck, turning the key to the ignition. He blew the horn, turned on the headlamps and rocked the truck back and forth. In the scattered light he could see dark red smears on the bear's fur. None of the injuries, so far as he could tell, seemed close to being fatal; he had struck the animal only enough to enrage it. The creature was standing directly in front of the truck. It was the angriest bear he had ever seen. Fanged and clawed, it was a terrifying image of doom. But Jack's instincts to fight or to take flight instantly converged, and he slid the gear into drive. He was about to press the accelerator when something behind the bear caught his eye. It was a cub, about sixty pounds, with white markings on its chest.

The sow jumped on the hood of the truck and smashed the windshield with her powerful paws. The claws missed his face by inches. In one fluid motion he flipped the gear in REVERSE and stomped on the gas pedal. The sudden shift caught the sow off guard and it rolled off the hood onto the ground. Jack wheeled the vehicle around and shot down the road to the highway. In his rear-view mirror, two dark silhouettes quickly retreated into the semi-darkness.

He stopped, a sudden fire flaring deep inside his chest. Tears blurred his vision and his chest heaved. He would be back there soon enough.

Next time, I'd better not see you.

When Jack reached the highway, he sped to the lodge to tell Dorothy the awful news. He pulled into the narrow path, and Dorothy covered her mouth in horror on seeing the shattered windshield and blood-smeared hood in the lit driveway. Jack called a friend to come stay with her while he reported to the police and rangers.

Half an hour after Jack left the ranger station in Deer Lake, a dozen local people were pulling into the lot of Bob's Big Stop Café in their half-tons, armed with shotguns and rifles. Dorothy and her friend were right behind them.

When she found Jack inside the Big Stop, Dorothy spotted the blood on his boots, and the realization struck—her son really was dead. Collapsing in shock, she struck and cut her cheek on a countertop. When she recovered, a policeman from Deer Lake took her to the town's night clinic for stitches and a sedative.

The Gros Morne park ranger, a young woman named Kim Hollings, showed up at the café. She had more questions for Jack. She couldn't think of a reason why the sow bear would attack Calvin or Jack. It was out of character for a bear, Jack conceded, except for one fact.

"The bear had a cub. Maybe two," he said.

"That's neither here nor there at this point," Kim said. "We have a problem bear and we will have to remove it. I'm sorry. I went to school with Calvin, although I didn't know him socially. I am sorry for both of you."

In the parking lot, Jack joined the group of hunters already organized for the removal of the problem bear. He was going to lead them, whether they liked it or not. He reloaded his 12-gauge and got into a truck belonging to another hunter. Behind them, a dozen trucks followed with their lights flashing.

They found Calvin's truck, and their headlamps reflected off the dark, shiny forms of the sow and the cub pacing about. The cub, as if on cue, ran for safety into the thicket. When Jack jumped out of the vehicle, the sow charged. Raising his semiautomatic, he fired, and fired again and again until she fell to the ground.

Ranger Hollings went up to Calvin's truck. The seats and dash had been ripped to pieces.

"I've never seen anything like it," she said to Jack as he approached. He nodded, then led them to Calvin's remains. When he was beside his son's body, he became confused, as anger crowded out his grief.

A man several yards away yelled to Ranger Hollings that he had found something.

"What is it?" she asked.

Jack ran over to see them examining a pile of leaves in the dark. The ranger slowly brushed away the debris to find a dead cub. A bullet hole—a rifle wound—gaped from its chest. Jack shone his flashlight about the trees, and a sharp, hot pain stabbed his eyes. This was the spot where Rick Preston had been. This was Rick's stand. Now Jack knew why the sow had attacked his son. There had been two or three cubs!

Rick had been the last hunter in this stand. The cub's fresh carcass confirmed that it had been dead no more than a few days.

Jack's thoughts raced, but one kept coming back to him.

That dirty son of a bitch!

2

The Dead and the Dying

The loss of his son through Preston's irresponsible behaviour was just the beginning of the bad news for Jack. While nursing his wife through her grief, he had to cancel the hunts and make preparations for the funeral. In front of Dorothy he would put on a brave face as he pondered their lives without Calvin, as a son, business partner and their only hope for grandchildren.

The next morning, while Dorothy lay in bed, sedated and sleeping, a policeman came up the driveway and greeted Jack on his front porch. He handed over a certified legal document addressed to Jack Crandall. It was from the Corner Brook Criminal Court. Jack signed for the document and began reading the summons.

With tears welling up in his eyes, a dull certainty settled in Jack that he was being ambushed yet again. According to the summons, the Parks and Wildlife Department was charging Jack for Rick's unauthorized kill. It stated that, as the paid agent of the client, under the law the outfitter or guide was responsible for the actions of his clients. It was therefore Jack's responsibility to see that his hunters followed the rules. It followed that any violations by Preston rendered Jack liable. Accordingly, he was to appear before court in two weeks to face charges for an illegal bear kill and for firearms violations. They wouldn't convict him for the shotgun in this province, Jack thought. But the cub was another matter.

"I'll fight them," he said to himself. "I'll beat them, too. The nerve of those bloody assholes!"

Meanwhile, his outfitting business licence was temporarily suspended. He would have to live off of his savings for the time being, an amount sufficient for the next several months, but not enough for the period of his suspension. And then there were the funeral expenses for Calvin. He gritted his teeth and shook his head. He would have to arrange for payment on term, meaning high interest on the loan from the funeral home.

After a time, he called the local funeral director, Norm Cotten, who made an appointment to see him right away.

Jack decided for the moment to conceal the document from Dorothy. His wife knew the penalty for those found guilty of such a crime. A conviction would mean the end of his business for a very long time. The news could not have come at a worse time.

When Jack arrived at Cotten's Mortuary and Crematorium, he found a brand new black Mercedes sedan and a hearse parked outside. Norm greeted Jack with a warm handshake, putting the outfitter immediately at ease. The mortician was a tall man in his thirties with wavy brown hair and a prominent gold tooth, dressed in a black suit and tie. The man impressed Jack as a professional, someone who was always looking out for a client. The two men passed the chapel and viewing rooms and turned down a short hallway. The hall led through a door, past a small kitchen and ended at Norm's office. Another hall led to the room where bodies were cosmetically restored while others waited for cremation or burial.

They sat in the small kitchen and Norm made coffee as he listened to Jack's dilemma.

"Now, don't you worry, Mr. Crandall," he said. "May I call you Jack?"

"Sure, Mr. Cotten."

"Norm. Just call me Norm."

"Sure, Norm."

"I have listened carefully to your story," said the director. "I meet many different people in all walks of life in my profession. I think I am a good judge of character. I like you, Jack. I believe you, and I may be able to help you. Here's the deal. I would suggest a closed-casket funeral, given the … condition … of Calvin's body."

"That would still be expensive," said Jack. "I was wondering if you had a payment plan?"

Norm gave him a pained look. "Don't worry about payment right now. Calvin was like a brother to me in the short time I knew him. What a guy! So intelligent! But, if it were up to me, I would go with cremation. Lots of advantages."

"I don't know. Dorothy might not like having the ashes around the house to remind her."

"Most people scatter the ashes at sea," Norm offered, "or at a favourite spot in the mountains or woods. Perfectly harmless. Very spiritual. And Calvin probably would have wanted it that way."

"But what about a headstone?" asked Jack.

"No reason why you couldn't also have a gravestone, too."

"I think I'll do that. Dorothy will go along with what I want for Calvin."

Norm offered the cremation and funeral without charge, and even refused payment for the cost of floral arrangements. Norm's generosity was something Jack least expected. He had prepared himself for hard bargaining from a man with such wealth as

Norm's. How else, Jack asked himself, could he make all that money Calvin believed he had?

"If you won't take payment, is there anything I can do in return? I insist, Norm," said Jack.

"Well … I could use some assistance around here, someone to help me with the funerals, digging graves and whatnot. I could even pay you a decent wage, more than what you'd make off-season. Close to what a plumber makes. I'd feel better, offering this in Calvin's memory. What do you say?"

Jack was overwhelmed and quite at a loss for words. Hours ago he had felt miserable, filled with resentment and distrust of this fellow. Now, observing Norm Cotten's smiling face before him, his faith in mankind was restored.

"Just until I can get my outfitting licence back."

"It's a deal," said Norm. "I can't tell you how much of a favour you're doing for me. I have had to dig graves myself in a pinch. Things are getting too busy around here for that, which is why I needed Calvin."

"I can understand that," said Jack.

"See me after the service," Norm said, standing up. "Take it easy, now. It's going to be okay."

The two men shook hands, then Jack hugged Norm in an uncharacteristically tender gesture.

"Calvin would have wanted me to help you," said Norm.

Calvin would have wanted to help me, too, Jack thought.

"The arrangements," Jack said. "How long?"

"Tomorrow if you like."

"Yes, let's get it over with right away. The sooner the better, for Dorothy."

"I agree," said Norm.

Following Calvin's memorial service, Norm delivered Calvin's ashes in a ceramic urn to the Crandalls. With sorrow in their hearts, Jack and Dorothy scattered their son's ashes away at the bear site where he had been attacked. The view had been Calvin's favourite.

The next day, in a cemetery in Deer Lake, Norm, dressed in blue jeans and a work shirt, was digging a grave. He laughed to himself every so often as he dug away. His laughter had the ring of vindication, the laughter of a supreme ironist, or a successful criminal, the secret laugh of a man who enjoyed winning at all cost.

He laid his shovel down for a moment and sat in silent reflection. So many dead, so few graves, so much to be done. With a sigh, he returned to shovelling. When he had finished digging, he lowered a coffin into the hole and filled it with dirt, stamping the surface smooth. He swung his shovel over his shoulder and walked to the nearby hearse.

Norm opened the door to reveal a cooler. In it were organs which would never see final repose, at least not in Newfoundland. The young man's body had just engaged Norm's time and energy when it was laid in its final resting place in the grave, adding a morsel to the island's natural food chain. The remains in the icebox, however, were destined for somewhere else. Getting behind the wheel, he checked his watch and remembered an appointment that he had to make after the last morbid business of the day was done.

An hour after sundown, Norm arrived at the funeral home. He studied himself in the washroom, then removed his jeans and shirt. After a quick shower, he donned his black suit and tie. In the mortuary room behind his office, he checked the refrigeration unit where he stored bodies for funerals and cremations. He pulled the sheet off of one corpse, a man in his mid-fifties, and inspected him, observing a long scar on the man's abdomen and bandages over his eyes. He likewise examined two other corpses, one of a man in his forties, another of a woman in her thirties.

The frozen winter ground had delayed a good number of burials of unclaimed individuals. Also, a cemetery chain in Cape Breton had gone bankrupt, leaving many bodies stored in county morgues, so many that the province had had to pay private funeral homes to store some of them, even as far away as Newfoundland. Norm had received ten bodies this way, over and above the natural deaths in and around Deer Lake. Most of the deceased, he made sure, were poor or elderly, likely to have no one claim them. When the deceased were unclaimed, the funeral home could legally cremate the corpses. Norm was holding a number of those waiting for authorization for cremation, but he had other plans to dispose of whole bodies and organs.

He locked the mortuary workroom and lowered its thermostat, then inspected the chapel. The cleaning service had left earlier that afternoon and he wanted to check on their work. Satisfied, he turned the page of his desk calendar in his office. There was one funeral scheduled for the next day, he reminded himself, and he would have to call to make sure all the flowers were delivered on time. Flowers were an expensive but necessary cost of doing business.

He was pleased with his plans for the funeral home, a business he had lucked into earlier that year. The previous director had passed away the year before, and his wife and daughter had moved to St. John's after his death. They had no one to run the business. Norm had lied to the widow. *Ah, yes,* he told the grieving woman, *I'll have my inheritance from my late uncle, and I can pay for the business in a year.*

Norm had received his mortician's licence only three years earlier, but he came with solid recommendations from his employers. He hadn't worked at a funeral home for more than six months, but who knew about that? In a year he would pay the widow a half-million dollars for the business. It would all be his.

The truth was that he had no dead, rich uncle. What he lacked in pedigree, luck and industry, he made up in guile. He discovered that faking cremations could be much more profitable. It was time-consuming for staff, and the energy bills for the hours of incineration were astronomical. For most other establishments, traditional funerals and cremations were the bread and butter for the directors, but not so for Norman Cotten.

His reflection reminded him that he had one last bit of business to attend to before calling it a day. He picked up a telephone in his office.

"Four more shipments for you," he said to the man who answered his call.

"What are they?" the voice asked. The man seemed all business, since he was one of those shadowy figures who regularly brokered special services from funeral homes and morticians, namely, the unauthorized traffic in body parts. As with most illegal trade, there was a heavy demand for the parts, for research and possibly for more nefarious purposes.

"Two males. One twenty-year-old, a bear attack, and the other eighty-four, Alzheimer's," said Norm. "A female, seventy-eight, auto accident, and a twelve-year-old girl, spina bifida."

"The organs in good condition?"

"On ice."

"Eyes?"

"Whole," said the funeral director. "Brains, glands, teeth, tongues. Anything else you need?"

"Gold fillings?"

"No, composites."

"Too bad," said the broker in a cool tone. "That would mean much more for you."

"I'm okay at twenty-five thousand for each harvest," said Norm, "but I don't want the parts here beyond tomorrow. I've had to dump remains when you couldn't get here on schedule. Its dangerous holding body parts after I've submitted certificates to the effect that they have been cremated. If you don't show, I have to do something with the remains, and to avoid a backlog, I've had to dispose of some in the woods. The kid who had worked for me since spring wanted to become a mortician, and he was always snooping, asking questions. Luckily he won't be working here anymore. So be here tomorrow."

"What happened to him?"

"A most unfortunate accident," said Norm.

"Auto?"

"No. A bear."

"Strange place, Newfoundland," the man said. "The hunter becomes the hunted."

"Happens all the time," said Norm.

"What do you mean?"

"Law of averages. You hunt, you're bound to have accidents. I didn't have time to salvage much of him; there was too little for cremation. I tossed his torso myself. It simply doesn't pay to turn the burners on. I am sure he made a good meal for the bears."

"I understand," the man said. "I'll be by tomorrow morning."

"Around eleven, preferably," insisted Norm, "but no later than noon. I have a new man starting. I don't want him to get suspicious."

"See you then. We have a ship scheduled for loading at the dock tomorrow, headed to the Gulf."

"That's where the buyers are?" asked Norm.

"Subcontinent."

"Okay. I don't really want to know. Bring cash."

"I always do," said the broker. "Have the conditions of death all documented for each package, coroner's reports labelled with each set of parts. No mixing organs, okay?"

"No problem," said Norm. "They'll all be in separate boxes."

On the way to his brand new Mercedes Benz, Norm felt very pleased with himself. Performing a quick calculation, he figured he stood to make almost one hundred thousand dollars by selling body parts instead of cremating them. Since he began supplying the black market, his balance sheet had greatly improved, and by the fall he expected to have paid for the business, months before the final note was due.

Norm Cotten figured that in five short years he could retire very comfortably, move to the Bahamas, and get away from this sordid business. And with the new man covering funerals and grave digging, he would have more time to pick the corpses clean of organs for his buyers. Visions of dollars piled high in his house danced in his head as he drove up the Viking Trail to visit his girlfriend, a young lady he had met in St. John's who was eagerly waiting for him to take her to the Halifax Casino for a weekend of R and R.

3

Brute Dominion

Before the court date, while Dorothy was away in town visiting friends, Jack sat alone on the deck of his back porch, holding his summons. He wanted to read the charges against him once more, but he was hurting inside. He gazed into empty space and wondered how long he could continue to stay healthy under the stress. Jack was in a funk, whether he would admit it or not, and his usual booster, Dorothy, was not with him. She made him act decisively when he might otherwise have been hesitant. He was looking at many possible choices, none without risks. Just knowing she was there would have helped him decide how to take care of the looming court case. Dorothy would have given him courage to act so he could focus on something else. What he disliked most was the feeling of dread that anything he decided to do would backfire horribly. And there was nothing now that he felt he could do. Sadness had a life of its own, and it came and went in its own good time.

The truth about Jack—if not a truth about all bouts of melancholy—was that his grief was relieved more often than not by rage. It was a therapy Jack had always taken great care to conceal from Dorothy, for he loved her dearly. But his temper was no secret to a great many other folks around the island who knew him. With his wife absent, he felt free to vent his dark side in profanity he would never have used in front of her.

Jack's rage festered, and it began to win the day. First came to him the apparitions of blood vengeance, and next, the heart-rending screams of his victim. It was all fantasy, of course, hideous fantasy, and cruel. The intended crime took place deep inside Gros Morne Park. It was winter. He had used a hammer, spike, and rusty oil drum to fashion a vicious trap, the same kind he set for bears. The drum had a punctured lid tapering downwards. It sat just below the surface of the ground. Jack taunted Rick Preston from a few feet away. The American was bleeding to death in the bear trap, whipped by the Arctic wind, begging for help. Jack revelled as he watched Preston writhing in pain. It was the justice of the wild, the justice of Gros Morne. He did not give Rick a *coup de grâce*. He watched him suffer for a very, very long time. Moments later, when the drama in his head ended in the demise of his victim, Jack's senses returned to him as quickly as they had left him.

Jack was filled with regret and doubt. The troubling thing, as he recalled his bloody fantasy, was how much Rick had sounded like Jack himself. Having never before heard Preston cry for help, how else could he know the sound unless it was in Jack's own voice? The person trapped in the drum, bleeding to death and screaming bloody murder, sounded eerily like Jack the time he had fallen down a ravine, breaking his leg. He recalled having screamed his lungs out at the time and that it took hours for his friends to rescue him. It was disconcerting, and he felt foolish and embarrassed now for having conjured up the gruesome images.

"I must be losing it," he said to himself. "There are other ways to get justice."

The real Jack, the Jack who was married to the sweetest, kindest woman in Newfoundland, vowed not to daydream again of Gros Morne justice. It would kill Dorothy if she even thought he had such fantasies.

Holding the service papers, he reread the charges, this time more slowly, and concluded that this matter was very serious, more serious than he had realized when he first received the papers. But since being served, he had not said a word about the hearing to Dorothy. Why, he reasoned, should he add his legal trouble to her stress? Besides, what if she absent-mindedly said something that ought to be kept in confidence and it got out to the wrong ears? For as much as he would never say it aloud, and as much as he adored her, he considered her far too trusting of the gossips around Deer Lake and Corner Brook. Why, if their men had done half the things the gossips said, Jack would often tell her, there would be no married men on the western side of Newfoundland. Yet, he could not keep his legal problem a secret from her much longer. Sooner or later she would find out.

Once again his temper reared its ugly head.

"How do you get off, Rick?" Jack began to ask, as though the man were present and not just a figment of his imagination. "Damned American! Once you got across the U.S.-Canadian border, you were scot-free. How about them apples! Incredible, isn't it? I'm the one being sued. Talk about insult added to injury. Well, they have messed with the wrong man."

No sooner had he made this declaration than a song from the Great War began to play in his head, inflating him with defiance. *See that valley over yonder. This is worth fighting for. See the cornfields of my father and of his father before him …*

Yes, this was worth fighting for.

He rubbed his chin, murmuring, "I need a lawyer."

Jack considered different lawyers he knew in Deer Lake or Corner Brook, but they all had something that ruled them out. Either the law office had a woman working there who knew his wife, or the lawyer was too damned expensive. He recalled that he had never had to think about legal expenses on this level before. How bizarre that he was facing any charges at all! But it was a serious charge. He had known outfitters ruined and jailed for the stupidity, greed or just bad luck of their clients. At the pinnacle of his career, rated by his colleagues and competitors as one of the best on the island, he had a lot to lose.

"Dammit," he said. "I didn't kill that cub. Why am I being charged? Why don't they go after the American? Why not prosecute Rick Preston?"

Jack shook his head, more frustrated than perplexed, because the same answer to his question kept popping back into his head. "Money, that's why."

He snatched the day's *Northern Examiner* from the table beside him. He was absent-mindedly scanning through the paper when his eyes fixed on a court news column. A name in the item had caught his eye: Nancy Cooper, Q.C. of St. John's. He recognized her name from his days in high school, someone he had rarely seen or heard of since. He hadn't known she had become a lawyer. Someone from his class was doing well. Good for her. According to the story, she had represented a fisherman in a Crown suit for overfishing his limit. Of greatest interest to Jack, however, was that she had gotten the charges against her client thrown out on a rare legal technicality. The Crown had not dotted all of its i's and crossed all of its t's.

She must know her stuff, Jack thought, *and she might be just the ticket for the prosecutors in Corner Brook.* "I don't have any problem with a woman as my attorney," he said aloud. Not if she fit the bill. And Nancy, good old Nancy, seemed like a winner. He reached for his telephone.

"Yes, Jack," said Nancy Cooper, "I'd say you need representation."

"Well, I'd like to see you as soon as possible," he said.

"I think we can set it up."

"What do you charge for a case like mine?"

"All depends on how much time I have to spend on the case, how many court appearances, travel, you know."

"Expensive?"

"At this point," Nancy explained, "it would be full-time work. Understand, there are no guarantees we'll win. But I'll need five thousand dollars as a retainer. If there's an appeal appearance, the fee could go higher."

"Ouch," Jack said. "Insult, injury and then I have to pay for it. Whew!"

"Think positively," she said. "I will have to see you tomorrow at the latest to get copies of the subpoena, the ranger report on the incident, and to get a statement from you. I take it you are pleading innocent to the firearms registry violation and the negligent hunting and outfitting charges?"

"Absolutely," said Jack. "I had no idea that the hunter we guided was a vicious and reckless man. On account of him, I lost my son. It was through his negligence ..."

"When do you have to appear?"

"In three days."

Jack could hear Nancy sigh.

"I think I can help you, Jack," she said, adding that she would fly out to Deer Lake and meet him at an associate's law office in Corner Brook the next day. "Don't worry about the firearms charge," she added. "It's going nowhere in courts these days. But three days before your appearance doesn't give us much time. I'll see you tomorrow. Meanwhile, I'll contact the prosecutor's office for disclosure documents, to review their case against you."

When Jack hung up the telephone, he felt calm, focused and confident for the first time since his legal woes began. It was the same state of mind he felt before what he knew would be a successful bear hunt. It was a feeling in his gut. It had seldom misled him. After talking to Nancy, he felt he could put the charges behind him.

Ah, yes, he thought. *Doesn't the anticipation of the hunt feel good!*

But he still had to tell Dorothy what was going on, and it was not going to be easy for him to find the right words to assure her everything would turn out okay. He was used to showing her his self-confident side, the Jack who was the take-charge, can-do guy to whom you leave every problem to take care of and forget about. Opening up to her about the suit could change her confidence in him, and that felt plain awful. But tell her, he decided, he must.

Dorothy entered the kitchen just before suppertime to find Jack sitting at the table. He had been expecting her for over an hour, prepared to let everything hang out. Now his courage left him. An intuition, perhaps, or merely the look of concern she gave him, stayed his tongue. He swallowed hard.

"What's happening, Jack?" she asked, her tone pleading.

He knew it was no use hiding it any longer. So he told her everything, about the subpoena, the charges that had been laid against him, but finished up on a hopeful note with the news that he had a heavy-hitting lawyer on his side.

"It'll be all right, Dorothy," he said. "We'll get it straightened out. But you've got to expect a lot of publicity. The next couple of weeks are going to be more stressful than anything we've ever handled before."

"Do you think you can win, Jack?"

"Yes, ma'am. But I know we have to be strong. I hate putting you through this."

"Don't worry about me, Jack. I can handle it if you can."

They embraced. Jack felt immensely fortified by Dorothy's attitude. He showed her the subpoena.

"Now, Mr. Crandall, is there anything else you haven't told me?"

"No, that's it."

"You're a good man, and you haven't done anything wrong."

"Yeah, that's what I believe, too."

"Jack, we'll get through this somehow."

"I guess I know my woman, too," he said, "and I think I've got the best one on the island. Don't you think so?"

"You are a handful, Jack," she said, grinning. "But I wouldn't want it any other way."

The following day in Corner Brook, Nancy Cooper met Jack in a colleague's street-level office, a former storefront on Main Street. Although they were the same age, the lawyer looked younger by at least a decade. She was tall and of slight build, with auburn hair, brown eyes and brilliant white teeth. Jack stiffened. This was not the girl he remembered from high school. She hugged him and offered her condolences.

A receptionist in her twenties joined the two of them in the office to take notes on a yellow legal pad. The younger woman, he thought, might know Dorothy, but she was probably too young to gossip with Dorothy's friends.

"What made the sow charge Calvin?" Nancy asked.

"Rick Preston," Jack said, "the American with my outfit. He had killed her cub. When she returned to the site for the bait, the mother remembered that her cub had been killed. Bears are very intelligent; they have sharp memories and they are highly unpredictable. When they want to kill you, more often than not they will kill you. I wish the sow had taken after Rick and—"

"Jack," she said, cutting him off. "The outfitter is responsible for ensuring that his clients obey the law."

"Yes."

She looked at him intently. "You did make sure the hunters knew the rules, right Jack?"

"Yes," he replied, "but I was miles away from the site. I could not be in two places at the same time. When they arrived, I held a briefing and outlined the rules and regulations for visiting hunters, including the prohibitions on drinking when handling firearms."

"Jack, after our talk yesterday I spoke with the investigators and Crown attorney's office. They faxed me background information, interviews with witnesses, that sort of thing. I'm curious. Did you know anything about Rick other than what was in his application to hunt?"

"No, why would you ask?"

"There was information in the disclosure documents. Did you know he had been charged with killing a cub in British Columbia five years ago on a hunt out there, and that he somehow beat the rap?"

"No."

"Did you know that a witness reported that one or two of your hunters had been drinking that afternoon at a local bar?"

"Oh, no," said Jack. "Why would they do such a thing? We gave them instructions on the legalities. They told me they were going for batteries and film."

"Had you observed them drinking heavily the previous day," she asked, "at the same bar?"

"Yes," he said, slowly, thinking of Calvin's concern over Rick's sobriety the afternoon before the hunt.

Nancy smiled to reassure him. "These are questions relating to your due diligence, Jack. The law requires that you check out your clients. The Crown could have some damning info on you. Would you object to taking a lie-detector test?"

"Of course not," said Jack. "I have nothing to hide. I'm telling the truth."

"Pardon me for a moment," she said, picking up her cellphone. "We'll have to arrange a session for you today or tomorrow." She dialled the police station and secured a time that afternoon.

Jack left Corner Brook feeling confident in his lawyer's abilities. That she was an old friend from high school further improved his morale. He slept soundly that night beside his wife and woke refreshed and ready to tackle the day.

He returned to the law office, and Nancy announced the results of the polygraph.

"Based on the test, you're not guilty of negligence causing death," she said. "You're a truthful man, and though the law may not see it that way, I'm going to call for a dismissal of the charges at the hearing."

In the public seating area of the courtroom, Jack spotted Ted Schultz the taxidermist, and a local bar owner. The Crown prosecutor, a man named Willard Turner, looked like American President Bill Clinton, with his red nose and smile. He was talking quietly to the two men.

So they're the state's witnesses! Jack thought.

The courtroom was full of reporters. The judge had subpoenaed the taxidermist and had given Nancy his testimony before the hearing started.

She was sitting with Jack, and Dorothy was seated just behind them. She leaned ahead and whispered, "I love you."

"I love you, too," Jack said, smiling. "You're a very smart lady. I guess I knew that when I met you."

Dorothy gently patted him on the shoulder.

When Judge Thomas Patterson entered the courtroom, the spectators and media in the court all rose. The judge read the charges against Jack. "Unregistered firearms and firearms violations resulting in criminal negligence resulting in death," he said. "The maximum penalty is a one-hundred-thousand-dollar fine and five year's imprisonment."

He asked Jack for a plea, guilty or innocent. Nancy, stepping forward, identified herself as Jack's attorney.

"Not guilty, Your Honour," she said, "and I ask that all charges against my client be dismissed. This province does not prosecute unregistered firearms. My client did not use a weapon in the commission of a crime. That charge should be dismissed. And there is no evidence that he was anywhere near the incident involving the shooting of the cub, resulting in a sow killing his own son."

"Your Honour," the prosecutor intoned, smiling, "you have the testimonies of a witness before you who accompanied Mr. Crandall's outfitting hunt. I have reviewed the testimony of the bar owner. He has given sworn statement describing the insobriety of the hunters. The law is very clear: The outfitter is responsible for the hunters and liable for any violation, indirectly, by them. I have entered the testimony of the other witnesses for the Crown into evidence, and because one of the prosecution witnesses is from a foreign country, I am requesting that the case be moved up to tomorrow so as to expedite this matter."

"Counsel," the judge asked Nancy, "is your client agreeable to a summary judgment?"

"Yes, Your Honour," Nancy said, "though I request that Mr. Schultz be placed under oath now."

"So agreed," the prosecutor said.

"What is a summary judgment?" Jack asked Nancy after court was adjourned for the day.

"The judge will decide the merits of the charge against you," Nancy said. "You won't need a jury trial."

"I don't know whether that's good or bad," said Jack.

"If there is nothing else that the Crown is charging you with, then we have a very good chance of getting a dismissal on all counts."

Court was scheduled for ten o'clock the following morning. The clerk administered the oath and Judge Patterson began.

"Thank you. Please be seated.

"Jack Crandall, will you stand before this court? The testimony you have given here, is it true, Mr. Crandall?"

"Yes, Your Honour, it is."

"Do you refute the testimonies of the Crown witnesses?"

"Yes, Your Honour."

"Well," the judge said after a short deliberation, "I find the charge of firearms violations and failure to register a firearm in this province unenforceable on the advice of the Attorney General. I will dismiss those charges. But let this court make it very clear to you, Jack Crandall, that an outfitter bears legal obligations that cannot be dismissed."

The courtroom erupted in protest. Judge Patterson banged his gavel. "Silence!" he shouted. "I want silence in this court!"

The room quieted again. "Thank you," the judge said. "Let me say, again, that what you have done, Jack, was culpable. And even though you were not present, you were responsible for the hunter's reckless disregard for the law. I am not going to dismiss the criminal negligence resulting in death charge. In this instance I move for the Crown. I hereby register a judgment of a fine of five thousand dollars for you and five thousand for each of the hunters in your outfit. That is thirty-five thousand dollars for your total fine. Your licence to outfit in this province is hereby revoked, as is your licence to own a firearm."

"We may appeal, Your Honour," said Nancy.

"So noted, counsel," the judge replied. Banging his gavel again, he announced, "This court is dismissed."

The courtroom erupted again with shouts and angry muttering—many of the onlookers from Deer Lake had travelled to Corner Brook that morning to support Jack and to celebrate his acquittal. The bailiff called to clear the court.

Outside on the sidewalk, Jack was trembling with rage.

"We can appeal," said Nancy.

"I should have asked for a jury trial," Jack grumbled.

"It would have been long and expensive," Nancy said.

From behind, Dorothy said, "We'll get through this, Jack."

"This has ruined us," Jack replied. "We may lose the lodge."

"Think about an appeal," said Nancy. "Take a few days and let me know. I will file one anyway. By filing, you won't have to pay a thing until it's heard."

At the lodge, Jack had a beer and went out to fish on the lake. He wanted to be alone; he felt that he had to nurse his wounded dignity, and he wanted to absorb his losses. Above all, he had to figure out what he should do next. He regretted the bad press, public humiliation and the loss of his good name. Second to that was the loss of his livelihood. Worst of all was that he and Dorothy were deprived of a future with Calvin.

The next morning, the story took top billing on all the radio broadcasts in the province and was repeated on the hour, every hour throughout the day.

4

Jack's Choice

A couple of days later, Nancy called Jack from St. John's to tell him that his appeal had been denied. Right then and there, Jack realized that his life was about to take another drastic turn. He would have to sell the lodge to pay the fines and Nancy's legal bill. Including the appeal, it all came to ten thousand dollars. While calculating his expenses, it occurred to Jack that he and Dorothy might have to relocate out west for him to start over.

Pouring himself a second cup of coffee and considering his next series of moves, Jack heard a crash coming from upstairs. Dorothy, her voice sounding feeble and faint, was calling his name. He ran upstairs and found her struggling for breath on the bedroom floor. Her pupils were dilated, and her face was pale and clammy. Jack immediately knew what had happened; she had suffered a stroke. Time was critical. He ran to the phone and called an ambulance.

"Take it easy, dear," he said gently. "Help is on the way. Try to relax."

His conjecture had been correct. At the hospital, surgeons performed an operation on her immediately. Dorothy had suffered a severe stroke caused by a clot in her neck. The surgeon spoke with Jack after the surgery and explained that she would be partially paralyzed. She would have trouble moving her left arm and working the left side of her body. Dorothy would recover some of her ability to walk, he added, and she would have to take daily medications.

Medicare covered much of the initial costs of Dorothy's recovery, but little in the way of her rehabilitation. The bulk of the cost of her therapist and a nurse were not covered. All too soon, Jack knew, he would go through his savings and be left deeply in debt. There was no way to avoid having to sell the lodge.

The sale happened earlier than he had originally anticipated, and they moved that month to a small cottage near Gros Morne Park and Lomond River.

Jack was resigned to working for the funeral home full-time, but this change came not without turmoil, anger and pain. Often he was prone to long, introspective daydreaming, thinking of Calvin and what it must have been like for his son when he worked there. He was often absorbed in the image of his son, wanting to follow Norm's example and become a funeral director.

"Jack! Hey, Jack!"

Norm had caught him standing in the centre of the morgue staring at a vacant doorway, a broom in his hands. Norm walked toward him dressed in his black suit and white shirt, a pen and pencil organizer protruding from his shirt pocket. He wore a bow tie and round, dark-framed glasses.

"What's gotten into you? You seem so distracted! You've got to pull out of it. I know it's hard, but …"

"Sorry, Norm. I have my good days and I have my bad days. I have to run an errand. I'll see you later."

Jack put the broom down, picked up his coat and started for the truck, thinking that he would stop in town to pick up some engine oil before returning to the funeral home.

Outside the auto supply store, he was putting a box of oil in the back of his truck when he spotted a familiar face coming out of the store. Rick Preston was carrying what looked like a pair of boots. Jack darted around to the back of the truck, trying to suppress the fire in his chest that had ignited at the sight of the man. He broke out in a sweat and began hyperventilating. To calm himself, he opened the box and stared at a can of oil, trying to focus on anything but Rick. Nothing on the label of the can, however, registered with him; he might as well have been staring into a black hole. He saw nothing, but he felt a great deal of hatred and pain. Slowly, he raised his eyes in Rick's direction. He was with another outfitter Jack knew, and it was obvious that they were working together. Nothing had been proven against Rick, so why wouldn't he be back, now that Jack was taking the heat? When Rick caught his eye, he quickly turned away.

That afternoon, Jack cleaned up the crematorium furnace behind the funeral home. He took a deep breath, determined to restrain the impulse to leave with shovel in hand and bludgeon Rick Preston. In his mind's eye he was doing just that, giving it to Rick with a *Take that, and that, and that, you dirty—*

"Daydreaming again?"

Startled, Jack came back to reality.

Norm patted him on the back. "Calm down, big fella," he said. "You're doing well here. Try not to think so much, and be strong so you can be there for Dorothy when she gets better. And she will get better, you'll see."

"You're right, Norm. Thanks for being a good friend."

"You're going to need a helper with these graves. I would

like you to oversee it. Can you do that for me, Jack? There'd be extra pay in it for you."

"Yeah, I sure could use the extra money."

"Fine, then. Oh, Jack, there's a delivery from the county morgue in the back of the hearse. It's to be cremated tonight, okay?"

"Sure thing, Norm."

It would be the last cremation for the day. The body in the hearse was a terribly disfigured old man who had been in an auto accident with a moose. The moose had smashed through the windshield of the car and torn the man's face apart. It was a depressing sight. The corpse, when Jack inspected it, turned out to be someone he recognized, a man to whom he had once sold some wood he had cut on his land—a Mr. Haywood, he seemed to remember. It was hard to believe that the old man was dead.

Jack's memory of him was still vivid, recalling hard and bitter disputes with the man. Nothing remained now, other than the bad memories. A dead body was worth next to nothing. He needed a break from work, fearing that if he did not leave he was going to strike out at someone in frustration. He knew he could not afford to do that at the crematorium.

Jack hopped aboard the hearse, not bothering to remove the corpse from the back. He drove up the highway, thinking he would spend half an hour in the park before cremating Mr. Haywood's corpse. At first he was thinking he wanted to free himself from any lingering rage. In a few moments, however, he was thinking of Dorothy, of helping her about, keeping her company and trying to make her feel better. Before he knew it, he was at the park turnoff and walking to the stand where Calvin had been killed. He had often visited this place for solace. Some of his son's remains were still there, buried under the twigs and leaves in a spot unmarked and unknown. His boy was already becoming part of the nutrients of the soil. Calvin's soul would be recycled or reincarnated into a living creature, as he had heard the Hindus believed. The clearing was tucked well out of sight in the forest and the path leading to it was shaded from the sun. Someone would have to be looking for it to find it.

When Jack stepped into the clearing, he saw a small black bear scamper away. A minute later, he saw it above him in a tall spruce tree. No more than twelve feet from the ground, the bear was so low that it could have jumped on him if it wanted to. Jack did not have a gun with him.

Unafraid, Jack uttered a low "woof." A few seconds later, there came another "woof" in response. A second cub entered the clearing, this animal no more than fifty pounds. It scrambled up the same tree. Both bears sniffed the air, and Jack figured they wanted food. One of the bears had a white star crest just below its neck, a marking that Jack knew well. The sight of the two bears revived pleasant memories of his hunting days, times when he would befriend and feed abandoned cubs with similar white markings. He would always lose track of time when he was around them.

Wearing a bemused expression, he left the bears and returned to the hearse, where the body of Mr. Haywood was lying in the rear. He opened the back door and dragged the body to the clearing. He stood behind the spruce, curious to see how the bears would relate to the dead man. He anticipated that the bears would be afraid to approach it, but he was not sure.

For a quarter of an hour the two bears did not move from the tree, although they never let him or the body out of their sight. The larger cub began cautiously, hesitantly, to slide down the trunk of the tree. Within minutes it had descended onto the ground and was circling near the corpse. The bear gently sniffed the air, pacing about. Then it approached and sniffed Haywood's body. The other bear began to lower itself backward along the tree, shinnying, just as children would down a pole.

The first bear suddenly lunged at the corpse and tore into the flesh. Jack stood motionless, trying to decide if he should attempt to stop them. But he was a seasoned hunter. He had stalked them too long to forget that there was always a danger in provoking any bear, adult or cub, whenever there was food between them and people. Not only were the two bears hungry, he had no weapon with which to defend himself. Despite their frail, famished appearance, Jack did not doubt for a second that the two young bears, a sow and the other probably male, would make short work of him if he interrupted their meal.

Jack watched in fascination as the bears ripped into Haywood's flesh. The corpse could not feel a thing, he reflected, inasmuch as death was the end of nerve sensation in any animal or human being. He recalled enduring as a boy what had probably killed something in him, too. Mr. Haywood was dead and could not feel a fang piercing his flesh, could not feel his flesh dissolving in the bear's maw. Jack mused that he had often torn flesh from his arms or cut himself without noticing any pain until someone pointed out that he was bleeding. Perhaps the beatings he received as a child had killed his receptors for pain, both physical and emotional. Maybe, he thought, that is why all he felt was anger overpowering what otherwise should have been grief.

Soon after the bears had stripped the man's thighs of flesh, the bear Jack assumed to be the sow turned around and scurried back up the tree, while the other left the corpse to nose around the far edge of the clearing. Jack collected what was left of Haywood, placed it in a plastic bag and made his way back to the hearse. Several urgent *woofs* soon followed closely behind him. He stopped and put his hands up.

The star-crested bear stopped and rested on its hind legs.

"You're still hungry, I bet. You want more meat, but you don't want me. You want what I have. But you're not big enough to take it from me!" The bear grunted and woofed at him once more.

It was time to get back to work and dispose of Haywood, or what was left of him. After making absolutely certain the bears did not show any sign of aggression, Jack turned his back to them and placed the bag inside the hearse.

He stopped at the turnoff to the highway. He had been tense before visiting the site, but the time with the bears had calmed him. He was grateful for the meeting and gave silent thanks it was not hunting season. If Rick could take a cub and get away with it, it stood to reason that another hunter wouldn't hesitate to shoot one or both of the two cubs Jack had encountered. A surge of anger coursed through his veins, brought to life again by the thought of Preston. He accelerated along the highway. Only when he saw a sign pointing to Deer Lake did he slow down to match the speed limit.

Jack wondered just how dangerous it was to feed human flesh to the cubs. Idly, he considered how naturally the idea had occurred to him. But a question was still unanswered. Would feeding bears human flesh condition them to wanting *only* human flesh?

He turned his thoughts to the task at hand. It was laughable, Jack thought; the ashes would allow the kin to remember Haywood, for all the good that would do Haywood. Ashes. Jack had already seen enough human ashes, and they all looked the same. Ashes are ashes. He figured he could easily replace the ashes of a person with the ashes of a dog and no one would know the difference.

Over the following weeks, it became a regular habit for Jack to visit the site where the two bears waited for him to bring them food. He brought them scraps of meat from the local butcher, along with doughnuts and other leftovers. Feeding the bears where Calvin was killed restored some of his spirit, and for this reason he felt it was fully worth the risks of a fine. The two bears, he came to realize, were a form of therapy to him. They helped him look to the future, to consider ways to recover at least some of his old self.

Jack always found them waiting in eager anticipation for his treats. There was a ritual to each visit. It would begin with Jack slamming his truck door to announce his arrival. The cubs, waiting in the same tree, would jump down as he greeted them with a customary "woof." When he stepped into the clearing, they would stand on their hind legs in front of him. They would eat meat from his hand and whatever scraps he tossed on the ground. They would grind and gnaw the pig, cow and caribou bones, the thighs, legs and ribs. When the bears had finished the meal, they each would sniff loudly. He would then give them bones and meat from butchered caribou which were otherwise destined for the compost heap or the garbage dump to be burned to a crisp. Caribou ashes. Grey flakes floating in the air. Ashes that could have been human as much as animal, for cremains all seemed the same. The ashes erased the source.

The visits stirred hope and brought Jack tranquility, self-respect and immense satisfaction. But on the drive back from the site, there were times the other Jack would return, the sullen and angry Jack who would curse Rick Preston, the taxidermist, the judge and the Crown prosecutor.

5

Man's Best Friend

In the crisp days of September, Jack visited the yearlings and watched them enjoy the treats he brought along. When anyone asked what he was doing with the meat scraps, he would say he had a couple of dogs. Whenever he fed the bears, he would watch in idle wonder as the two voraciously ate the offerings. There was little else now in which he could take pride. It was a relief to him to feel that he was providing for two orphaned bear cubs. It was nice to be needed.

Not a day went by without him thinking of Calvin. The treatment he had suffered by the courts further aggravated him. Sometimes he would stop while performing some task and flush at the memory of his trial. Images of the arrogant prosecutor would come into his head and he would become lost in rage and despair as he replayed the court appearances. Then, the bears would calm him. In the woods, he would find a total escape where the past no longer weighed on his mind.

The larger of the two bears, he guessed, was the male. It was growing fast, and from its height, stride and paw impressions, he figured it weighed one hundred and fifty pounds. The boar had a thick coat, black punctuated with a small star-shaped patch. Its black, spongy-tipped nose glistened with moisture. It had two opal eyes, alert and shiny, and a low forehead. Jack noticed also that it paraded boldly in front of the other bear, clearly a sign of male dominance. Indeed, the smaller of the two seemed to follow timidly behind its sibling, a deference common with female bears. How odd, that the slight difference in animal design gave way to a major difference in function, a contrast so great that it was rare for anyone to see the bear gender roles reversed.

Jack's hunting stand was starting to disintegrate. Signs that any hunting accident had occurred were long gone. The bait-scented trees—green spruce, fir and pine—still bore the remnants of ropes once strung up high between the branches. Jack had put them there to hold the scent bags many seasons past. Now he saw that the bears had selected and staked their claim to one large fir tree as their home. The claw marks and torn bark on the tree, for all Jack knew, could have been bear news or bear poetry.

As the days became cooler and September neared its end, the bears learned to compete for Jack's attention and for extra scraps of meat. They would approach and prance about in front of him, in expectation of the food he threw to them in the clearing. He would call and coax them, stroking and rubbing them. Soon he was able to do something that surprised and greatly pleased him. The bears would let him touch and hold their paws. Not only was he able to stroke and scratch them on the backs and shoulders, but he was also soon examining their paws, extending their legs, jostling and playing with their ears. At times he would push and roll the bears on the ground, and they would seem to have as much fun as any kids, woofing and snorting all the while.

He did not doubt that he had established an intimacy with the animals. He could now shake hands with one or could grab it by the snout and firmly slap its shoulders and back. The bears would rub against his leg the way cats often do with their owners. Even so, there were limits to their intimacy. They only let Jack play with them for a little while. He couldn't embrace or hold them down very long before they became annoyed. After letting Jack toss them on the ground, the larger one would jump back and dash at him, growling loudly, zigzagging and standing on its hind legs to grab and sink its claws into Jack's woollen jacket. For an instant, the boar had a fearlessness about him that brooked no challenge. Meanwhile, the second bear would merely dodder to the tree, shinny up and meekly look down from a branch twenty feet above the ground, as though it feared something unhappy was about to take place. Jack would assert his dominance at that time by picking up a branch from the ground and slapping the big one on the nose, which was sure to elicit a submissive "*woof*."

The male would plant his paw on Jack's shoulder, stunned by the sharp blow, while Jack would say in a deep bass, "No!" It would drop its paw and, as if on signal, Jack would drop the branch, open a pail he had been carrying, pull out a piece of bacon, moose, or chicken, and extend it with his open hand.

"Here!" he would say. "Take it!"

Jack would keep coaxing the animal in his deep voice, until the bear licked the flesh and nibbled at it, gulped it down and then licked Jack's hand with its rough tongue. The other bear, either taking courage from the larger one or finding the handouts too enticing to resist, would soon shinny back down the tree. It would sidle over to Jack and pace nervously around him, begging for its share of the meat, too.

Jack didn't know what to make of the bears when they raced about him. All he figured was that he must have given them a sense of security; otherwise, they would have retreated to the treetop or another hiding place. But he knew the day would come when the bears would see him quite differently.

"Imprinting," he said to himself. "I must imprint them with fear and respect for me."

Jack began from that time onward to condition them to respect him. Like every good hunter, he was under no illusions that he could teach or train the bears. Ever since the dawn of animal domestication, people learned to condition them to respond to human cues. But one could never rely upon conditioning alone. Until a breeder finally achieved a domesticated strain of the beast, there was the possibility that a conditioned animal would revert spontaneously to wild instinct. Indeed, many a bear or lion circus trainer had lost life or limb when the animal failed to respond on cue. Wild beasts could simply break free of the simple carrot-and-stick conditioning to attack the person who had raised, fed and cared for it since birth.

It was with the aim of establishing his authority that Jack would slap the bears when one of them tried to sink its claws into his pants or tried to climb up his leg. His slap was firm, not meant to harm, but merely to discourage the aggressive instincts of the bears. The blow would be delivered with just enough force to focus the animal's attention. And, a few days after he had started the conditioning, both bears were responding to his "No!" and "Get it!" commands. The program made the bears now eminently manageable, following the ancient Egyptian proverb, that to manage a child or an animal requires the discipline of the rod, until the child or young brute accepts authority. The bear was one of the easiest animals to condition when young.

One day, to try out his control, Jack even brought a moose hide for them on a tether. Taking some flesh scraps, Jack smeared them on the hide and said in his deep voice, "Get it! Get it!" The large bear hesitated for a moment before leaping on the hide with its mouth open and grabbing it. For days Jack would drag the hide behind him shouting "No!" in order to get the bear to halt its attack. Later, he merely had to raise his hand so the bear could see it. The bear would instantly release the hide and look at Jack for its next command. "Good bear," Jack would say, feeding the animal a piece of pork or beef. "Good bear."

For the better part of an hour, Jack would repeat the exercise. One bear would gorge itself on scraps, the other would watch, and then it too would be put through the same routine. Jack would then feed both bears the final morsels left in the pail. Occasionally, he would attempt to control their hunting instincts by conditioning their reaction to stray animals that happened to come nearby. He would issue commands and offer rewards to reshape their behaviour as they stalked and harassed their quarry, before they died of exhaustion or fright trying to escape.

He never pampered the bears, nor tried to cuddle with them. Once he had won their trust, he sought to control them, to make them obey with a simple command, to get them to retreat and to play for food. The play, for that was all it meant to the bears, would entertain Jack for the duration of his daily visits. While he was with them, he seldom felt sorry for himself anymore, nor did he feel as sad about his son.

A few days before the first major snow in October, Jack began leaving large heaps of garbage food in the clearing for the bears. They gorged themselves and buried the meat that they did not eat. They were no longer soft-nosed adolescents. Moreover, the female seemed almost as bulky as the male. The two bears still nuzzled Jack, as they had in the summer, but they had grown less affectionate in the fall. They growled more often and no longer tried to follow him. Where once their claws had seemed fat needles sticking from the tips of their paws, they were fast becoming like cruel-looking horns. Often when Jack approached the bulkier one with the star-like crest, it would make a rush at him, a fierce flash in its eyes, ears flattened, only to stop cold in its tracks a few feet from him, turn around and canter around the corner to a clearing in the brush. The tactic showed Jack that the bear already knew how to bluff a foe, how to backtrack on a hunter and how to ambush him with lightning speed.

Ambush was the modus operandi of bears on the attack. They were superb hunters, and like the large pythons or anacondas of the tropics, they captured their prey by lurking at hidden points along their intended victim's trail. The bear, having encircled Jack, would give his friend a reprieve. In the next breath, it was thrashing and crashing back into the clearing. When it returned into view, it sat on its hind legs, dangling its tongue out like a little boy or girl joshing an old man.

Jack's inspection of the bear's ambush path revealed a devious preparation. The path had already been cleared: the animal had removed all twigs, stones and other debris from the ground that would have made any sound that would betray its advances. The hunter on the bear's trail would not have heard its paws, would never have detected its breaking a twig or crushing a leaf on the ground. The path the bear takes to surprise the hunter from behind is swept clean beforehand. Some call the bear intelligent for preparing exit trails in its territory, and they marvel at its foresight to engineer a defence that man would have had to discover and circumvent. Bears know how to hunt by instinct alone, and for most of mankind's history, instinct has given this animal the edge. Jack believed his bears were unaware of the reason why they cleaned their paths, just as they were unaware that the offal Jack fed them each visit was intended to control their behaviour.

All indications that fall had pointed to an early but severe winter. There were hardly any days when it rained, and no black frost showed in October. The summer insects of the forest fell silent in due course, while only the squirrels continued to forage among the vegetable- and insect-infested debris and the green pine cones. Wild fowl left the island. Crustaceous lichens on the rocks of the Lomond and Humber river shores stopped spreading and turned brown. It was a fall of active rutting, and moose were calling, the preliminary to duels for the favours of cows.

Jack recalled an image of the larger bear late that October hanging over a branch in a tree, while its sibling lay in a nook at the base of a large dead maple for winter hibernation. The smaller of the two had managed to squeeze through the narrow entrance created by a knoll and the rotting tree, its small den covered by debris of the forest floor. Every time Jack roused it, the bear growled and quickly pushed its bottom farther into the den.

One evening, when the snow was falling gently and it was still easy to follow the path to the site, the bear's only response to his intrusion was an indignant snort. The yellow full moon was already looming over the trees. The cold wet wind from the ocean whipped through the valleys. The memories of the past spring burned hot and painful in Jack. His bitter losses haunted him then, a solitary man tramping through the freshly falling snow in the dark. In a rage, he began muttering curses and oaths of revenge while on the pathway to his truck.

The first major snow fell for thirty-four hours straight, burying the forest floor. Much of it melted in the following days, but it was only a foretaste of the much heavier snowfalls to follow. The first of the Labrador polar storms blasted in around the first of November, and two days later, when the temperature dropped well below freezing, all signs of the yearlings had vanished. After the first week of snow, Jack saw his bears no more, but the snow showed claw prints of other bears in the area. He also noticed, much to his alarm, that these strange prints had been made by large adult bears. The safety of his hibernating yearlings concerned him.

There were no long thaws after that blast of frigid weather. The snow packed up an average of six to eight feet, while the wind from the Gulf of St. Lawrence hit seventy miles per hour. The Arctic gusts bent trees into the horizontal growth of tuckamore, stripping bark from evergreen tree trunks and cutting right into the inner cores of the naked wood. The winds were so strong and so sustained that the trees hit by the blasts along the shores were bent inland and partially uprooted. They seemed frozen in motion, as though they were running away from the ocean to the protection, deep in the valleys, behind the mountains, of Gros Morne.

Late March saw the first signs of spring, and the days grew longer. Purple, white and red crocuses poked through the snow. In early April, wispy clouds collected in rings about Gros Morne Mountain. Jack found the larger of the bears, somewhat trimmer than in the fall, gorging on insects and grass and digging around the site where Calvin had been lost. The bones of a moose he had given them in the fall were nowhere to be found. Jack paced about the clearing.

He stopped. A few feet from the path, he noticed something dark. To his horror, he saw it was the ravaged form of the bear he believed to be the female. It glistened evilly on the wet ground. Upon closer inspection, he saw that it had indeed been a female, and that her neck had been broken and chewed open. Chunks of fur lay scattered about her, evidence of a vicious struggle.

Her companion sniffed at Jack and nibbled at his pants.

"It's all right," Jack said. "I am sorry, my friend. I know what it's like to lose someone dear." He felt sad as he set about burying the female where she lay.

Jack ate his lunch in the truck on the way back to the crematorium. When he arrived, he found Norm in the furnace room.

"Two more bodies for you," the director said. "And when you take care of those, I want you to clean up around here. It's beginning to look like a garbage dump."

Jack felt his blood pressure rising. The place was in disarray because of Norm's penchant for storing in the furnace room the effects of the dead he buried. Cleaning and straightening up the mess would take all night, and he knew Dorothy would need him before he finished. But if he neglected to clean the room another night, he would further annoy Norm, who seemed more and more irritated with him lately. Jack sighed and went to work.

6

Marking Territory

The start of bear-hunting season fell on the same day Jack read of two bear attacks in Gros Morne National Park. There were no fatalities, but what caught his interest was the spokesperson for the park. It was the ranger named Kim. He had not seen much of her after Calvin's funeral. Because of her job, she had surely known when she saw him that he was going to be subpoenaed. Yes, it made sense for her to avoid him. Poor thing! What could she do for him? Still, it would have been nice, he thought, for her to have called when Dorothy had fallen ill.

The Western Gazette newspaper out of Corner Brook had quoted Kim Hollings on the front page: "We think the bears are mating and the sows are out and about with their cubs; that's the reason for the latest attacks. People have to exercise caution in the park. Bears are unpredictable."

Jack studied the accompanying photo. Yes, Kim Hollings, that was her name. She was trim, black-haired, pretty, with a rosy robust face. She wore her ranger uniform and hat, the epitome of efficiency and detachment. He wondered if she was married.

In the days to come, Jack saw Kim's image more and more. There were reports of a fifty-percent rise in the number of bear maulings in the park and surrounding area. Multiple killings by bears the next week in the park brought the number to six. Parts of the bodies had been consumed before the victims were discovered. Aided by volunteers and hunters, the park and wildlife wardens removed seven bears and took them away to be destroyed.

One photograph in *The Western Gazette* stunned Jack. It was none other than Rick Preston, and he was standing over a full-grown bear, his rifle in hand. Jack was furious for the rest of that day. He felt defiled at the injustice of it. While he shuffled around the furnace of Norm's crematorium mopping up, and while he tried to take care of his ailing wife at home, his son's killer was enjoying the limelight. Jack, the fall guy, along with at least two other innocent people, both of whom he loved dearly, were all victims of one man's criminal negligence, and that man was Rick.

"It doesn't matter to him," Jack muttered to himself. "The man is living in a nice home on Long Island with his wife and kids. He is a stockbroker making lots of money." While he fumed, he noticed that he had just crumpled the newspaper in his hands.

A thought simmered and boiled over. "I could," he said. "I could." But he quenched the flames inside him when he thought of Dorothy, who still needed him. Oh, but he could, if only he had the chance to get away with it. Crushing the newspaper into a ball, he slammed it into a wastebasket in the corner.

Soon the radio stations began reporting bear attacks almost every day. They usually occurred late in the evening or at nighttime and were mostly directed at campers. The park and wildlife service for Gros Morne issued reports to the press the first part of the week denying that there was a crisis. Nearly everyone Jack came in contact with was aware that the initial reports were meant for damage control, to prevent the national media from noticing something odd on the island. The park assured the press that the frequency of reported attacks was no cause for alarm, but locals in and around the park knew better. The attitude of some of the townspeople was cynical when it came to the government, and in and around Gros Morne and Deer Lake the talk was that something had to be done before the attacks got out of hand.

In May, a tourist from Switzerland was attacked by a black bear in his campsite while he was cooking a trout, and died the following day. Two days later, a garage attendant was attacked behind his garage. He had run for a tree, but the bear pulled him down and broke his neck. When he was found, half his abdomen was missing. Two young men were killed by a bear the following day in a park picnic area on a local river, twenty miles away from Deer Lake.

A toddler was almost snatched from a mother's back pouch when she was walking to her car in the grocery parking lot in the centre of town. The culprit was described as a small young bear that didn't even reach the woman's shoulders. The report said that when she saw it running toward her, she charged at the bear, with her baby still on her back, and she kicked the animal in the nose. The bear's own charge bowled her over on her side, but it had had enough of the fierce mother and scampered off. The woman became a media heroine as the foiled attack got the attention of the press throughout Canada and North America. But that heroic episode was quickly eclipsed in the media coverage.

The very next day, there were two more fatal attacks. The Corner Brook newspaper reported that Jessie Black of Deer Lake, the reigning queen of the Lomond River Golf Club's par-three, sixth hole, was mauled to death on the green. The avid golfer was just about to pot her tee shot in the tree-lined course, when the bear raced across the field and flattened her. Her caddy fought with it, chased it away by using her driving irons, but she died on the way to the hospital. The seventy-four-year-old woman was a mother of fifteen, grandmother of twenty-seven, and great-grandmother of ten.

In its lead editorial, *The Western Gazette* called on the provincial government to send in a special investigative unit to find the reason for the problem bears. TOURIST SEASON IN THE TOILET, the editorial's headline read.

> We continue to let our provincial government off the hook. If the premier doesn't take real action soon, there will be no tourist season this summer.

The Northern Examiner newspaper further reported: BAD-ASSED BEAR NEWS: IT'S BAD, REAL BAD. Quoting one outfitter, the *Examiner* wrote,

> This is the most serious blow to the industry since the 9/11 terrorist attack. Locals have reported cancellations of ten family fishing trips up the Humber River this summer. Booking agents report other groups of tourists have also cancelled. Something must be done to crop our bears and remove the problem ones. The federal government should assist the province. Is anybody at Natural Resources listening to the bodies falling?

Less sarcastically, Parks Canada issued a report the next day in response to the editorials, reassuring the residents of western Newfoundland.

> There is a larger than usual number of young bears in and around Gros Morne National Park, and the number of panhandlers have also increased during the spring.

> Familiarity breeds contempt. A uniquely high number of bears have become especially aggressive to people, and Parks and Natural Resources officials will be cropping a large number and removing any problem ones. To assist in this effort, the hunting season around the park will remain open all year.

At the funeral home the day of this newspaper report, Jack met Norm with a young man he didn't know.

"Morning, Jack," said Norm. "This is Mark Hughes. He's our new employee. I'm getting him to do some painting inside this morning, but I'd like you to take him to the graveyard after lunch."

"Hi Mark," Jack said. "I sure hope you have a strong enough back for this job."

"I know you, Jack," the young man said. "Sorry to hear about your son. I don't mind hard work—besides, it will help me keep in shape for hockey this winter."

"By the time the ground freezes, you should be able to drive the puck through the net, " Jack said. "Shovelling is good exercise, that's for sure."

"Jack," Norm interrupted, "I have two bodies in Stephenville for you to pick up. These two were killed last evening when their car hit a moose. Their families say they want them cremated. Can you get to that after you show Mark where to dig the graves?"

"Not a problem, Norm."

The rain let up by lunchtime, and the sky was a leaden grey as the two employees walked to the hearse to double-check the tools they would need to dig graves.

"Well, Jack," Mark said as he walked alongside the older man, "you seem to be in high spirits. Your feet are hardly touching the ground."

"Thanks, buddy, for telling me how well I'm feeling."

"Yes, boss."

"Okay, Mark," said Jack. "Follow me into the graveyard."

Jack showed him the plot that Norm had staked out for them. He instructed Mark where to pile the earth and how to set the box in the ground to hold the casket.

"It's almost four-thirty," Jack said after he was satisfied Mark could handle the rest on his own. "I must go and pick up the bodies in Stephenville."

Mark shook his head. "You're something else, Jack," he said.

"How so?"

"You're the best outfitter on the island, but they've got you digging graves."

Jack was quickly becoming irritated at the brash, talkative young man.

"I've got work to do," he said, not wishing to follow Mark's line of discussion. "Digging graves is not what Norm pays me for. That's why we hired you."

"Norm hired me, not you," Mark said.

Jack let that pass.

A couple of days later, Jack piled some garbage and meat scraps aboard his truck. Forty-five minutes later, he turned off the Viking Trail and drove into the site to meet his bear.

Half an hour into his visit, the bear seemed to have grown intoxicated from all the scraps Jack had brought. He was about to tell the animal to finish its meal, when he heard a noise. The animal tensed as well and stopped frolicking. Jack got up and looked down the path to his truck, but saw nothing.

It could have been a moose, he thought, *or a squirrel.*

Without warning, the young boar rushed down the path as though in full pursuit.

"Help! Help!" a voice cried out from down the trail a few moments later.

Jack followed the bear's path through the trees. He stopped about fifty feet from the animal after it came into view. It had pinned a terrified Mark Hughes to the ground.

"No!" Jack barked.

The bear withdrew at once.

The shaken man rose to his feet, brushing himself off.

"You followed me," Jack accused him.

"I didn't mean to," said Mark. "I didn't mean anything, really."

"How long have you been here?"

"I arrived a few minutes after you got here."

"So you've been tailing me, huh?"

"Well," Mark said, "Norm asked me if I knew where you went in the afternoons."

"Norm?"

"Yeah, Norm asked me the other day."

"So what are you going to tell him?'

"Well," said Mark, "nothing."

"Oh yeah?"

Jack took a step toward the bear, and pulling a piece of scrap meat from his jacket, offered it to the animal.

"You know that's against the law," Mark said uneasily. "You know they're saying the bear attacks are happening because people are feeding them."

"This meat is garbage," said Jack. "No one cares."

"If you say so, Jack." Mark turned toward the road.

A panic button went off in Jack's head.

"Get him!" he shouted.

In an instant, the bear crashed into Mark's back, knocking the wind out of him and pushing him to the ground.

Mark screamed in a shrill voice.

"No!" said Jack. "Stop!" The bear had been conditioned to obey, and it responded immediately to the command.

Jack didn't trust himself at that moment. He had reacted on impulse, on an instinct to survive, when Mark had turned his back. Mark was in danger, as much from him as from the bear.

"Get outta here, Mark!" he shouted as soon as the bear let him go.

Mark rose quickly, eyeing the animal. Clearly annoyed at this show of defiance, the bear came at him again. It knocked Mark to the ground, picked him up and tossed him about. The bear was having fun; it did not use its teeth or claws on its new plaything, and twenty minutes later, a bruised Mark was lying prostrate on the ground, bleeding from scrapes on his face and hands. The bear stood on all fours, panting over him.

"Go!" Jack said, commanding the bear, but when the young man started to rise, the beast went into action again. It was treating Mark as if he were nothing more than a chicken or other small animal Jack often employed to entertain the bear.

"Please, Jack," Mark screamed. "Get him away! I don't care what you do. I don't even know you! It's just a job."

"No!" said Jack, stopping the bear as it dropped Mark once more to the ground. This time Mark lay still, hardly breathing.

"Go!" Jack repeated, horrified at what he had witnessed.

The bear ignored him and sniffed Mark. This time it lifted him by the shoulder. The doomed young man screamed as it raced through the woods, dragging him in its maw.

A few minutes passed in shocked silence. Jack was almost afraid to breathe as he waited in the clearing. Finally, the bear returned to the site, playfully pulling Mark's limp form behind it. It released the young man's shoulder and let him fall to the ground. It rolled him over with its snout, sniffed again, and licked its trophy.

There came no response from the crematorium's newest employee. His eyes were frozen open with fright.

Jack rushed over to Mark and pushed the bear away. He held the man's wrist, and he was not surprised to find he had no pulse. He performed emergency respiration, and still Mark did not respond.

Jack sighed in frustration. Why did Mark have to follow him to the site? There was no way he could leave the body here for someone to find. He had to dump him somewhere.

Thinking fast, an idea took shape in Jack's mind. He would take Mark and the bear back to the cemetery. There he would drop the body and walk the bear around enough times to leave visible tracks. As he put his plan into motion, somewhere in the back of his mind he registered a detached awareness that he had crossed a line from which there can be no return.

The Northern Examiner carried the news of Mark's death two days later. In an effort to avoid public anxiety, the Newfoundland government withheld the true cause of this most recent tragedy.

MAN'S BODY IDENTIFIED

> The Deer Lake detachment of the RCMP have identified the man found dead in the cemetery at New Ferolle on Wednesday, May 22. He is twenty-year-old Mark Hughes of Deer Lake. No cause of death was released. Based on the coroner's preliminary report, an RCMP spokesperson said that he appears to have died of natural causes.

PART II

7

When Bears Attack

On the tenth floor of the National Parks and Wildlife Building in Ottawa, a meeting was taking place. Four big game animal biologists were listening to the mysterious findings of a colleague from Newfoundland. The man's trim, youthful physique and professorial manner suggested a college graduate student. But Dave Bishop was a seasoned Ph.D. and had been a provincial biologist for fifteen of his forty years. He was based in the Wildlife Department's Deer Lake office. The four men were clustered at one end of the large meeting table while Bishop talked, illustrating his comments using a projector. In his right hand, he held a control. On the white screen on the wall behind him was projected the image of a black bear, rendered faint by the bright fluorescent lights overhead.

The Newfoundland species, *Ursus Americanus*, was ranked more intelligent than any other bear in the world. It was larger than its cousin, the more docile North American black bear; indeed, on average it was as large as a Rocky Mountain grizzly. Of late, it had become a threat to the half-million residents of Newfoundland by virtue of the multiple bear attacks on the province's west coast. The number of incidents was of crisis proportions, with attacks reported even in town centres. The most baffling aspect of this crisis was that the number of moose and caribou herds, the bear's favourite prey on the island, had also risen. Because of the bear's abundant food supply in the forest, the biologists at the Parks and Wildlife Division reasoned that bear attacks against humans should, if anything, have declined.

In seasons when the forest seemed an inexhaustible provider for wild bears, there were no attacks on people at all. Dave Bishop's theory was that the genes of the beast had changed with time. Now, he said, they were as aggressive as grizzlies. Both types were omnivorous, feeding on vegetation nine days out of ten. All the more curious, he told his colleagues, was that the bears had started to hunt down humans. Although traditionally the grizzly was the most feared bear of North America, the Newfoundland black bear now had to be considered more dangerous.

He speculated that one possible cause of the early-season attacks was that visitors to the island had been feeding bears the previous season and during the winter when some had come out of hibernation prematurely during a thaw. The visitor problem was further complicated, he added, by the excessive bear/people ratio, and the tendency of parks like Gros Morne, desperate for revenue, to let too many people and vehicles into the nature reserve. Anti-hunting activists also contributed to bear overpopulation.

"Can't they see that properly managed conservation policies can ensure that animals will survive human contact?" Dave said.

Alex Hagen, the senior federal biologist, spoke up. "That's right," he said. "Hunters depend on bears, so they work hardest to see that the population survives."

"Another thing," said Bishop. "We need to better educate visitors to the parks. Many of them believe every bear is Smokey or Gentle Ben."

Most of the killings, he went on, were taking place from the north of Deer Lake through Gros Morne Park and as far south as Corner Brook. The fatalities had all occurred in a one-hundred-mile radius of Deer Lake itself. Obviously, he added, the animal had to be cropped in regulated kills through an expanded hunting season, without endangering the survival of the breeding stock.

The federal biologists agreed to form a joint task force with their provincial counterparts to deal with the emergency. Each was assigned a specific area in Gros Morne's seven hundred square miles for six months. Before the meeting was over, Alex Hagen agreed to coordinate the federal contribution to the task force. Dave Bishop bade the feds goodbye and caught his flight to Deer Lake.

Dave arrived at the Gros Morne ranger station late that afternoon. Besides the office building, there was a separate bunkhouse with a kitchen, which would be his home for the next few months. Another building was used for storing bulky equipment such as traps and cages.

Bishop changed into a pair of blue jeans and a gingham shirt with the sleeves rolled up, and pulled on some hiking boots. Many might have mistaken his casual dress for a lack of maturity or thought that he was simply unprofessional, but the man had a rugged disposition. His face reflected an intense mental alertness and a focused gaze. He was all business, ready, decisive; there wasn't much around him that went unnoticed. He bore obvious marks of experience: bronzed knuckles, broad calloused hands, a right arm sporting a long, white scar from wrist to elbow, and on his right hand, tiny holes filled with white scar tissue, the badges of his outdoorsman credentials.

Dave walked to the office door and found it unlocked. There was no one in sight, so he sat down at a spare desk and sized up the room. The walls were covered with maps stuck with dozens of location pins, and the room was strewn with documents, field equipment and chairs. On a worktable were a telephone, fax, scanner and computer with a video camera next to it.

He was staring vacantly out the window when he heard a woman's voice from behind.

"Hello."

He turned around.

"Kim Hollings, sir," the woman said. She was dressed in the Gros Morne park ranger uniform. "I'm filling in for the ranger for a few months while he's out on disability."

Kim extended her hand, which was small and calloused to his touch. The two knew of each other through their work, but they had never met on a personal basis and had never been formally introduced.

In profile, she reminded Dave of many Greco-Roman paintings and statues. She had the smooth forehead, straight nose and delicate chin of a classic female bust. But she also seemed to have a great deal of energy and confidence. She looked like a lot of fun, he thought. The ranger's green hat covered most of her black hair, the brim throwing a shadow against her suntanned face.

"Dave Bishop, from the Deer Lake Wildlife office. I just flew in from meetings in Ottawa. I'd like to inspect the bears in this area."

"We are starting to take a few, almost every day. You must be exhausted," she said, peering into his face. "A long flight?"

"No, but it's been a long day," Dave said, stifling a yawn and grinning. "I'm fine."

"Maybe its just red-eye," Kim replied. "If you like, I can brief you in the morning."

"No, now is good. You don't look like a girl who handles bears," he lightly teased. "I'd never have expected to find a gal here as a ranger. It's tough work."

"I have no problems with them. I studied them in college and in my wildlife management programs. I've had a lot of contact with bears during summers here on the island.

"Have you ever been chased by one?"

Kim shook her head. "No, but I have backed off a few that I've stumbled upon in the park. They leave me alone. "

"Then they don't have very good taste."

"I'll take the compliment," she said.

"I'd like to go out now to look at some trails," Dave said, "and inspect some scat."

"I'll come with you," said Kim. "Meet me outside in a few minutes at the jeep next to the front door. I have to fill out a form. It won't take long."

The vehicle's back seat was filled with ranger's equipment: a shovel, a tool box, a medical emergency kit, maps, a spare gas tank, an oxygen tank and camping equipment. There didn't seem to be much room for Dave's camera bag and the lab equipment he would be using to test the bear excrement. As he was standing and looking through the side window of Kim's jeep, trying to figure how to make room for his bags, he suddenly sensed her presence behind him. Much to his surprise, she had changed her clothes.

Kim was still wearing her ranger hat and brown suede trail boots, but now she was wearing tight, dirty jeans that accentuated her long legs and gave her curves in all the right places. She had replaced her green shirt and black tie with a mackinaw shirt. This was hardly the outfit Dave had expected a sub-ranger to wear on a bear expedition in the park.

"Ready?" she asked. She reached down, picked up both of his bags and went around to the back of the jeep.

"I might get smelly," she said, noticing his curiosity about her clothes. "I won't have a spare uniform until next week."

"I'm not complaining," said Dave. Her change of clothes made sense. The bear excrement he wanted to inspect could require some kneeling and sitting on the damp ground, if and when they took it from a trapped bear.

"I'll help you with those, Kim."

They rearranged the clutter in the back of her jeep, squeezing and piling the gear tighter until there was room for his bags, and slammed the back door shut.

On the way, Dave observed Kim glancing at the scar on his forearm. He was used to this, so he didn't offer to explain it.

"That's not a knife cut," she said finally.

"No. The light strip is scar tissue."

"Bear?" she asked.

"I'm afraid so."

"A big guy?"

"A small sow," he said, "in a snare near a road in the northern part of the park. We had her under sedation, she was coming to, and we almost had her free."

He fell silent.

"And?" Kim asked.

"A tourist pulled up," he said.

She waited for him to explain what he meant, but he did not. Instead, he started to adjust the buckle on his camera strap.

"What did the tourist do?" she prodded. "Frighten the animal?"

"No," he said, in a slow, reluctant tone. "The guy was trying to help us. He had stopped along the road to watch us. He walked over and offered to help. Said he was used to handling cattle, being a rancher from the States. But while he had our attention, the bear came to life, and the snare was open."

"Tourists are nuts sometimes." Kim said.

"Sometimes," Dave said softly.

They parked the jeep several miles up Lomond River from the station. In twenty minutes, they found a round fecal clump a few hundred yards up the trail near a stream. Dave took a photograph, recorded some data on his small tape recorder, and removed a sample of the scat. He was the model of efficiency and experience, and Kim was left to hold his bags. While viewing the specimen through his small portable microscope, he recorded the location and time on tape. When he had identified the sample, he sealed it in a vial, marked it and stored it in a box in his gear bag. At that time of year, he knew, the bear's diet is mostly vegetation; much of the rest is carrion, from the bodies of dead animals.

"It's mostly derived from meat," Dave said. "It is darker than scat from vegetation. The lab will be able to find out from the DNA if it's human. Bears don't digest food long enough to destroy all the ingested material."

"Yep," said Kim. "Fifteen minutes from mouth to scat."

"A bear can gorge itself for hours," said Dave, "so long as there is food in front of it."

There was a lot of guesswork in the art of visually analyzing bear scat; field methods were still not advanced enough to make more than an educated guess. But even if flesh were in the scat, he might not be able to conclude that it was human flesh without conducting DNA testing. The reported attacks may have occurred for no reason, other than people feeding the bears and leaving garbage around; whatever the cause, they had clearly lost their fear of people.

Dusk was approaching; they knew it was not safe to search for samples and trapped animals after dark. They hurried along to their next stop, a bear trap near the river.

The trap was a simple one. It was constructed of two steel oil barrels welded into a large pipe tube. The tube was wedged precariously between two posts in the ground, having been pulled nearly free of them. The trap bore large indentations in its steel frame. Loud thumps from inside the trap indicated an animal not at all resigned to its fate.

"It moved the barrels," Kim said gleefully.

"Only a bear could have the strength to do that much damage," said Dave. "Let's see what we've got."

They found that the bear was a good size, most certainly an adult. It was facing away from the trap door, unable to turn around. Dave unrolled a tarpaulin on the ground near the trap door. He quickly jabbed the animal's rump with a hypodermic syringe on a stick, its plunger attached to a folding arm to squeeze out a dose of tranquilizer. The bear thrashed about trying to swat the stick, but it did not have enough manoeuvring room to hit it. Dave checked his watch to calculate the effect of the tranquilizer. A few minutes passed in silent waiting.

"It's licking," Kim said as she looked through a slot at the other end of the trap. "Almost under."

"Maybe. Let's wait," Dave said.

In a minute, at the other end of the trap, Kim found little response when she poked at the bear's mouth through the slot.

"He should be under now," she said. Slowly, she raised the trap door, revealing the animal slumped into a heap. They had precious time to lose before it came out of its sedation.

Dave checked the bear's breathing to confirm that it was resting and breathing comfortably and that it was in stable condition. One could never be too careful sedating a wild beast. It was never the same as dealing with captured animals in a lab or a zoo, where one could observe them from behind a cage for protection. There was also the danger of overdosing the critter before one could weigh or measure it; there was an art to estimating how much knockout juice could be safely injected.

"It can't have been in there for more than a night," Kim said. "That was when we set the trap."

She and Dave each grabbed a hind leg and together pulled it out of the trap to measure the animal's head size, claw length, pad spread, dental condition and weight. Dave read the measurements into a tape recorder. His examination showed it to be a male. He read the bear's vital signs: pulse, blood pressure and breathing. Meanwhile, Kim gripped a pair of calipers and carefully measured the animal's testicles and penis. The organ was erect and thrust well forward beyond its foreskin sheath.

"Let's hope he's a sound sleeper," Dave quipped.

Once the measurements were taken, Kim quickly tattooed a number on the inside of the bear's bottom lip.

Dave took out a pair of dental pliers from his gear bag, inserted the pincers behind a lower incisor tooth and pushed the tool down into the gum to get a good grip. Slowly, gently, he worked the premolar free and deposited it into a marked clear plastic bag. He filled a syringe with enough blood to fill a vial for testing. In the most delicate stage of the examination, he put on surgical gloves and extracted a sample of stool from its rectum. He secured the sample in a sealable plastic cup and placed it in his gear bag along with the vial of blood and the premolar.

Dave attached a plastic tag with a wire and crimp to the bear's ear as Kim held it. At the same time, she monitored the animal's breathing closely. It had been unconscious less than fifteen minutes.

"You're very efficient," she said.

"Experience," Dave said. "I have no natural abilities at this."

He adjusted the stiff leather collar of a small radio transmitter. Placing it around the bear's neck, he set the signal to a satellite receiver and locked it.

Standing, he said, "Let's get out of here."

Twilight found them again on the trail, headed in the direction of Kim's jeep. The two glanced around nervously as they walked, each fully aware of the danger involved in walking through bear-infested woods at night. The trees to their right opened upon a stream about twenty feet away, and they saw two bears drinking its waters.

Suddenly, the larger animal charged from the stream through the alders, head down, lip curled in hostility, only to swerve a few yards away from the top of the trail and off into the brush. The other animal at the stream, meanwhile, had disappeared.

"Uh oh!" Dave exclaimed.

"It's only a couple of black bears," Kim said. "For goodness' sake!"

Dave stopped. He was about to say he thought he heard a twig breaking, when one of the bears suddenly darted from the brush behind them. It bowled into them, staggering Kim with a blow to the head. The force of the impact also threw Dave forward, landing him face down on the other side of a ditch, where he rolled several yards from the trail. He could hear Kim shouting loudly, "Get away from me!"

Dave lifted himself, half-dazed. Fir tree needles poked his face and clothing. Immediately he abandoned all thought of retrieving his gear. His first priority was to help Kim. Racing blindly across the bottom of the ditch through a clump of interlocked spruce, he pushed his way through the brush. Branches of conifers tore flesh from his already raw face and hands. He knew that he had no time to lose.

When he climbed back onto the ridge, he saw the bear a few yards away. It was standing over Kim on the ground. It began dragging her by the foot; it was taking her away from him and toward the thick alders on the side of the trail.

More out of desperation than any conscious plan to rescue her, he screamed as loudly as he could, "Get away! Let her go!"

The bear stopped pulling Kim. It raised its head in the direction of the man's voice. It saw no known rival in him, no threat, so the dark mass huddled over Kim again, grunting and snorting, and clamped its mouth back on her leg.

Dave began to walk toward the bear, shouting as the animal hit at Kim with its paw. It picked her up by the shoulder and threw her five feet away. It woofed, gave a low growl and stood up, its jet-black eyes fixed on Dave. When Kim started to edge away from the spot where she had landed, the animal forgot about Dave and jumped back on her, grabbing her forearm.

Dave advanced, wielding a large unfolded utility knife he always carried, drawing the bear's attention once more.

It charged him; it must have realized that Dave would be stopped no other way. In a second, the beast swung its paw and slapped Dave's right wrist with it, sending his knife flying. Now it had him, a man, the bear's enduring enemy, disarmed. There has been a primordial struggle between bears and men begun when the two first met in the ancient forests; now Dave and the animal were locked in the latest skirmish. This time the bear meant to prevail. It swatted him to the ground, then rolled him over and over on the trail, as if he were a toy doll. All the while, it tried to slash at his face, but he managed to get his arms up each time to fend off its deadly claws.

Kim scrambled to her feet and yelled for Dave to play dead. The bear stood up on its hind legs at the sound of her voice. It struck Dave with a paw, launching him four feet away, and rushed in to bite his shoulder.

Suddenly, it stopped. Just as it was about to sink its teeth into Dave, there came a woof from the brush. The sound had come from the other side of the stream, from the other animal they had seen. Their attacker retreated, then raced away in bulky, bow-legged jumps into the far brush, toward the stream and the other bear.

Kim stumbled over to Dave. She had escaped with a heavily bruised ankle, claw marks, and bite marks on her forearm. Dave had shallow bite marks and claw marks, but was not harmed otherwise. Supporting each other, they limped back to the truck. The adrenaline still surging through their veins, they swapped nervous laughs, downplaying the close call. They had to get to the medical clinic in Deer Lake, but they had the presence of mind to stop and look around to gather up Dave's gear. Evening and night sounds of forest creatures and the piping of a lonely jay were the only other signs of life as they gathered the equipment.

"We just had to run into a sow and cub tonight," said Dave. "What luck!"

"We'll have to let the police know."

"First," Dave said, "the clinic."

"Rabies boosters," Kim agreed.

After visiting the clinic and police station, they returned to the safety of the ranger station and nursed their bandaged hands, arms and shoulders. Dave sat on Kim's living room couch, holding a cup of tea in his free hand. Facing him and sitting in a brown chair, Kim sipped a glass of orange juice.

"You need anything?" she asked.

"I'm okay. A report of the attack on us will probably hit the papers tomorrow."

He was perplexed, full of questions about the frequency of bear attacks that month.

"There have been too damned many of them. This isn't natural," he said.

Kim agreed. "Something is provoking them to target people."

"In the first week of the month," Dave said, "there were four attacks, the second week five. So far, there have been nineteen attacks reported, with eight fatalities."

"Twenty attacks," she corrected him, "as of tonight."

"Something's wrong," said Dave. "They don't attack this frequently. There are rarely more than a couple every few years."

"An old high-school classmate of mine was killed last year by a bear," Kim said. "And he was a hunter, the son of an outfitter."

"I remember that guy. Calvin something."

"Crandall. His father is famous. But he lost his licence, everything."

"Yes," he said, "I know the details. Tough, huh? Were you still in contact?"

"Oh, no. I seldom saw him when I was in college, unless it was in passing to say hello."

"Everyone knows everybody around here," Dave said.

"My life is the name Gros Morne," Kim said. "It's my real name, I think."

Dave raised his eyebrows.

Kim laughed at Dave's reaction. "My life has been gross," she said, "and it is often dismal and gloomy."

"It can't be all that bad."

"I know," she conceded. "The earlier settlers certainly had it rougher here."

"Kim," Dave said. "Would you like me to hang around with you awhile, for company."

"Yes, I'd like that," Kim replied.

Dave felt awkward. He thought he should stay to cheer her up, but he worried she might get the wrong impression. She had suffered the roughest of the attack. The truth was that she had probably saved him. A life-threatening attack like the one they had just gone through was the kind that created a special bond.

He was equally certain that the bond had nothing to do with romantic feelings. Theirs was a friendship forged from the intensity of a daring and dangerous encounter; he felt they at least needed one another's company for a while.

"Alex Hagen and his crew will be arriving tomorrow," he said. "Do you think you can supply us with more vehicles by then?"

"I can arrange that. Two more provincial biologists are coming in from Corner Brook tomorrow," Kim said.

"It's very pretty on the coast."

"That is the saving grace of this place for me."

"Is there a hamburger joint on the way?" Dave asked. "The guys will be starving."

"Yes. Bob's Big Stop Café. It has dynamite burgers and fries."

"We'll all be working closely together, Kim, for the next six months or so."

"Looks like it. What do you think?"

"Well," said Dave. "Despite our most recent adventure, we have a chance of getting this thing resolved. I love every part of this park, every bit of coast, every lake and alpine plateau, although the flies and mosquitoes are murder right now, and I have never seen underbrush so thick in all my life. The tuckamore is near impossible to walk through. The bears make their own trails under the brush."

"This is the only place where people walk on top of pines," Kim said. "It's magical, and the only way to trek around the hills with tuckamore is along the bear trails."

"You could cut a path yourself," Dave said. "Hunters go around lakes and bogs, and loggers' woods roads."

"It will be difficult," she said, "to track the bears that attacked us."

"We might trap them, but I'm sure they're not the only perps. The island has almost twenty thousand of them."

It had been a long day followed by a traumatic evening. Dave got up to leave. "We will talk more in the morning," he said.

"Thanks, Dave. See you then."

Dave retired to the bunkhouse, and with the help of a painkiller, slept until sunrise.

8

Dinner Guests

A few days later, Dave was sipping his first coffee of the morning in the ranger's office when the telephone rang. Kim answered and passed the phone to Dave. It was Alex Hagen, with some interesting news.

"It's weird," Alex said.

"What do you mean by weird?"

"Well, it's the stool sample we found in a hay field over on Route 430, up from Deer Lake about ten miles. The scat's fresh and there's some bone in it."

"What!" Dave exclaimed. "That's impossible. There hasn't been anyone reported killed in the past week."

"Well, that's not all," Hagen said. "We collected some in the park yesterday and it had flesh in it. The scat we found at another site contained only grass or buds."

"The bone might tell us something. Let's see if we can confirm whether it's human," Dave said.

"We've been looking at the places where people went missing late last fall," Alex continued. "There were a few in September, and it was within a ten-mile radius of where we found the samples. We were wondering if there was any way that the bears didn't finish their kill, and went back to their stash after the snow left."

"Well, that sounds reasonable," said Dave. "But I think we'll send these samples to the St. John's laboratory. I'm sure the labs there can tell us the age of the other scat. We'll get them over in the chopper. I'll call to alert the lab.

"Good work, Alex. Let's see if we can find more specimens in other locations tomorrow morning. Then we'll trap some bears and test everything: their teeth and blood, and how much fat they have. I even want to check their brain size. We'll need to hire experienced hunters to assist us."

"Right," Hagen said, and hung up.

This was grim news, Dave thought.

"I'd hate to write that we have bears eating human flesh," he said to Kim. "We don't have any missing persons. It makes us look bad."

Dave felt the bears in the park had to be cropped soon. He was a man of action, and in a crisis a man of action does not hesitate to act. A few hours later, he met the team of scientists at Deer Lake and discussed with them the plan of attack. The first thing he wanted to do was organize and lead a hunt, to kill as many bears as he could. That was the thing to do. Examine the scat, check for human remains, the whole nine yards. The others were all for it. Dave had another idea to float by the task force.

"We need to post a bounty," he said. "Two hundred bucks for each snout."

It was a scheme to encourage hunters, in hopes that if enough bears were killed, the remainder could be isolated enough to end most of the attacks.

Stung by complaints it was not doing enough, the provincial government announced that it would adopt Dave's suggestion to enlist hunters in the bear cull. The news delighted Dave; the more bears killed, the better. The good press made his personal stock soar in the public eye. *The Northern Examiner* reported that he was the hero of the bear attack suffered by Kim and himself, not the other way around. Life was never fair, he admitted guiltily to himself, but what could he do? Write a correction to the paper?

A fax from the lab in St. John's reported that the scat found the day of Dave and Kim's attack and the sample from the trapped bear were negative for human remains.

"Why, that's good news!" Dave told Kim after he helped get his team of biologists settled in.

Favouring her ankle, which was still sore from the bear attack, Kim collapsed into a nearby chair.

"You're recovering?" Dave asked.

"I feel okay," she said.

"Oh, I forgot to tell you. I'm thinking of going fishing on Saturday morning. The lake is just beautiful," said Dave, smiling, "and it's full of trout. You could use a break."

"Ok," said Kim. "I'll go."

While they were fishing the lake on Saturday morning, Jack Crandall was casting his rod on the Humber River. He had been fishing for only a few minutes when he hit a four-and-a-half-pound grilse, a salmon that he could legally keep. If it had weighed any more, he would have released it to the river, in keeping with the law of conservation on the island.

He cleaned the fish right away. While doing so, he decided he would try his luck with a big salmon he had seen roll farther down the pool. He picked up his things and decided to try his luck there.

"That's a taker if I ever saw one," he whispered to himself as he saw the salmon's back breaking through the surface. He cast and pulled the fly toward the salmon. Immediately, the fish struck hard and Jack almost lost his grip on the rod. The reel screamed as yards of line flew off it. The reel became hot to the touch. This was a fresh one, and wild as hell! It took Jack downriver while it fought, and it jumped four feet into the air several times.

For a split-second the line went slack, then the salmon made another dash; the line snapped and the trophy fish went free. Jack sighed.

Nothing had moved in the river towards midday, and the air was hot and humid, so Jack decided to give up. A few minutes later, back at his truck, he began removing his vest and boots while sitting on the edge of the seat. Just then, his bear stepped out of the clearing, walking on all fours over to the bank where Jack had left the remains of the grilse. As the animal began to eat, Jack climbed out of the vehicle and approached it. The bear paced around him, still licking its chops.

"You were watching me the whole time, weren't you?" he said. "You are not safe here. You will have to come with me."

He returned to his truck with the bear following a few paces behind like some pet dog. Jack opened a pail on the passenger side of the truck, pulled out a stick, jabbed a piece of moose meat from the pail and turned to the bear.

"I don't think I need this," he said. "But I don't want you to run on me."

The bear gobbled down the meat, then Jack opened the door to the back of the truck. He lured the bear into the truck, coaxing it by tossing more moose into the back of the truck. When the bear was inside the cap, Jack closed the door and opened the small side windows for ventilation.

Back home, he let the bear out and tethered it to a post behind his shed. Dorothy stepped out on the deck with her walker.

"Was that a bear?"

"Yep," Jack said. "I'm taming it. It's no problem."

"A bear! Imagine!" Dorothy exclaimed. "We have a bear! Oh my! They're attacking people and he wants to bring one home. Oh, my nerves!"

Without a word, Jack went back to his truck and held up a salmon. He smiled at his wife, hoping that this would placate her.

Dorothy's face lit up. "Good!" she said. "Your trip wasn't a complete waste. You caught one for me. I was hoping you'd catch one, so I waited to eat with you. My mouth is watering for the taste of fresh salmon! I'll start the barbecue. But, Jack, please lock that bear back in the shed."

"Okay," Jack said with a grin. "It doesn't bite, unlike salmon. Fought a good-sized one for ten minutes before it broke my line."

"I can only imagine," Dorothy said. "Want a beer? I put a few in the fridge awhile ago."

"Sounds good."

"The first salmon of the year is always the tastiest, don't you think?" she asked.

"I'll drink to that," Jack said.

That afternoon at the ranger's headquarters, Alex Hagen and the task force examined more new stool samples collected earlier around Deer Lake and Corner Brook. The samples from the city were filled with grass and buds, but the samples found east of the park contained what appeared to be meat.

Dave studied the map on the station's wall. "These samples are from different bears," he said, pointing at the map where the earlier samples had been found. He compared it to the samples found that day.

"There's no way a couple of bears could go from here to way over there," he said. "Not at this time of year."

Though no one could explain the differences, they all agreed.

"I'm hoping to get us some bears next week," Dave said, still pointing at the map. "The ones near the road to Big Falls should be right in the middle of these samples that we're finding. Maybe we can discover something."

Just then the telephone rang.

"What's up?" Dave said into the receiver.

"We have trouble," Kim said. "My patrolman in the park just saw four large bears cross the main road."

"What's wrong with that?"

"The bears were on their way to a campground that's full of boy scouts this weekend."

"Oh, shit! Get there as quickly as you can!"

"You're a lot closer, Dave," Kim said. "Unfortunately, I'm in Deer Lake, about a half hour from you."

"Come on!" he shouted to Alex and the others, slamming down the phone.

They jumped into the trucks Kim had provided from the park fleet. Dave sat in the passenger seat of one and dialled the police.

"Get everyone you can in vehicles at the campground right away!" he shouted. "Get them to blow their horns and make as much noise as possible. We have four bears heading that way!"

"Yes, sir," came the sharp reply.

Dave called the ranger based at the northern end of the park.

"We may need your dogs at the trailer park."

"On my way, Dave," the ranger replied.

Dave looked at his driver. "Pick up your speed a little, will you? We're about ten miles away."

"Yes, sir," his colleague said, flooring the pedal. They zipped past the other two trucks.

His cellphone rang again.

"Dave, it's over." It was Kim.

"What do you mean it's over?"

"I just spoke to the police. The bears made a mess of the scout tents. They were looking for food, but there was little to eat. The boys were scared, but these are boy scouts. They know the rules. The food was hanging between trees out of the bears' reach, so they gave up."

"Are there any casualties?"

"They're not sure," Kim said. "They have to do a head count. Two of the bears had something in their mouths, but it wasn't human, thank God!!"

"I'll be there shortly," Dave said, and shut off his phone.

"It's over for now, so you can slow down a little," he said to his friend.

When they arrived, dozens of young boys were standing around looking shaken but otherwise unhurt. Some of them were crying, while others were picking their things up off the ground. Plastic and paper littered the campground. The rangers, scout leaders and a few of the troops were trying to untangle the tents. Most of them had been torn down.

"Anyone missing?" Dave asked the scoutmaster.

"No. Three boys were out on bikes on the main road, but we can see them heading back this way."

"Good! We're lucky so far," Dave said. "I'd rather see a mess like this than a life taken."

"Thanks, gentlemen," the scout leader said to Dave. "We can clean this mess up in no time. That was some kind of surprise for us! What should we do about tonight? Is it safe to camp, or do you think the bears will come back?"

"You could put up some electrified wire," Dave suggested. "It would be better than nothing at all. The bears might not be so pleasant the next time they discover you're the only food around."

"That's a good idea," the leader said. Turning to the scouts, he said, "Let's do it, guys! Maybe we could put some brush on the inside for camouflage so it won't look so much like a war zone."

Dave shook the scoutmaster's hand. "I'll have someone stay and help you," he said. "With any luck at all, you should have it in place by dark."

"Perfect. Thanks."

As a further precaution, Dave advised the scout leader to call a supply store in Corner Brook and order air horns for each scout to carry.

"What a war!" Kim said a little later, when she was alone with Dave back at headquarters.

"Yeah, we got lucky," he said.

One of Alex Hagen's staff brought in three samples of fresh scat found near the trailer park.

"Good work," said Dave. "Let's check out this scat, right here."

Dave saw immediately that the scat was dark brown, with no signs of animal hair, which would have been present if the sample had come from a moose or caribou or another furry animal. The colour of all three samples suggested the presence of flesh.

He studied the map again in the makeshift lab.

"Two of these bears could be our perps. They may be feeding on a carcass buried somewhere," he said. "But where did the other two come from? I don't know about you, but I'm totally confused. What a day! We were lucky we didn't lose some of the boy scouts."

Dave was still tense. The public wanted answers, and he felt his good reputation was tenuous at best.

The next morning, far from the ranger station, Jack was mowing his lawn. He was sweating pretty hard by the time he finished, so he got a beer from the fridge and went to sit on the deck where Dorothy was relaxing.

"I think I'll take a nap," she said after a long silence.

"While you're napping, I'll go check on the bear," Jack said as Dorothy rose and went inside. He collected a pail of scrap meat from his truck and carried it to the shed. There he found the animal still asleep, but it soon rose when it sensed meat.

Jack laid the pail down just inside and slammed the door shut, locking the bear inside. He figured it would go back to sleep after the meal.

He returned to the kitchen to find Dorothy sitting at the table, instead of asleep in the bedroom. She gasped and turned pale at the sight before her.

"Jack, did you cut yourself?"

He looked down at his trousers. There were spots of blood on the legs, below the knees.

"No, that's chainsaw oil," he said quickly. "I didn't screw the top on tight."

"Well, it sure looks like blood. I didn't realize oil could be the same colour."

"I'll take them off," Jack put in quickly. "I'll scrub them down later in the shed."

"You'd better," Dorothy said indignantly. "I don't want that stuff in my washer! Throw them out and get a new pair."

"Sure, they'd just get messed up too! It's better to use old clothes. I can't seem to keep clean."

"The bear is dirty," Dorothy said. "The bear is why you can't keep clean."

With shaky fingers, she poured out pills from different medicine containers on the table. Jack went to the sink to pour her a glass of water.

"You mustn't get excited," he said. "You don't want a relapse."

"Sometimes," she said, "I can't help but get upset. I was hoping you'd get rid of that bear. Do you think you ought to keep it, I mean, with all the things going on?"

"He's fine," said Jack.

"Did you give it a name?"

"I was thinking 'Starlight.' How's that sound?"

"It does have a star on its chest."

"Yes," he said.

Picking up that morning's *Northern Examiner*, he saw a photograph of a group of hunters who volunteered to crop bears in the park. His face turned red. He flung the paper on the table, got up and went out of the house.

Puzzled, Dorothy picked up the newspaper. On the front page was a man holding a rifle and standing over a bear. She recgonized Rick Preston of Long Island, who had just killed his fifth bear for the Parks Department.

9

Victims' Rights

The bear attacks in the first half of June levelled off to three a week, only one of which was fatal. But people were still alarmed. There were outbursts of hysteria among the women while the men voiced anger and frustration. Still the provincial government did not announce an emergency, and the public recriminations and finger-pointing increased. Everyone in the know felt that business as usual was not going to work. There were signs of a lapse in public confidence; some were buying high-powered rifles and ammo and carrying them without firearm permits. Rumours and protests in the media abounded that there was bureaucratic rivalry between the park administration, the police and the park biologists.

A few families of attack victims filed suits against the Gros Morne National Park management, and in the natural course of such things, the victims or their families gave the standard and predictable press interviews accusing the park officials of negligence in protecting visitors from bears. Once the lawsuits were announced and the families had gone public, of course the park administration clammed up.

All the tension came to a head after a bear attack on two boys during broad daylight in downtown Deer Lake. The announcement that the park management was reluctant to release information on the downtown bear attack that June day led to a firestorm of public protest. Many officials called in sick rather than report to work and confront angry protesters.

The two male victims of the vicious town attack, Jordan Barney, twelve, and Ansley House, fourteen, as reported in *The Northern Examiner* the next day, were near a popular fishing creek in Deer Lake. Around midday, the two youths were just downstream from a road culvert when a bear came out of the alders on the opposite side of the brook. Sighting Jordan, the bear chased him for about ten yards, knocking him down and biting his neck until he was dead. Having finished Jordan off, it went after Ansley, knocked him down, inflicting bites to his head, stomach and face. Having satisfied itself with Ansley, the bear then went back to Jordan's body and dragged it through the culvert and into the brush. A woman from town who was turning off the Viking Trail to go down the main street pulled over in time to see the bear mauling Ansley, but by then there was nothing the terrified woman could do. A half-buried carcass, identified by police as Jordan, was found the next day about a mile and a half from Hodden Memorial Recreation Complex. Ansley was able to relate how the attack began before he died, four hours after the mauling.

The local rangers and police called for volunteers to track the "problem bear" and kill it. The usual procedures in such cases were followed, with tracking stations positioned around the site of the attack and traps set up around garbage dumps in the area. Extra patrols were put out at night. The federal biologists with Dave and Kim were assigned to the incident as well. When reporters from *The Western Gazette* and *The Northern*

Examiner tried to get reports of the attack, they were blocked by officials.

The families of the dead boys hired solicitors, filed for release of the report and sued the provincial management for "gross negligence in Gros Morne National Park and surrounding area, which includes Deer Lake," so the affidavit read.

The Northern Examiner headline on the attack the next day screamed, GROSSED OUT AT GROS MORNE NATIONAL PARK BEAR LUNCH. The pun was obvious; most readers understood it was a jab at the park managers. The public was furious.

A town meeting organized at a local church by the boys' families was attended by a large number of residents—more people than actually voted in most elections. Provincial government officials and the mayor, a former policeman and fireman, went to the meeting. He found it difficult to get a word in edgewise, since every time he tried to respond to a question, someone called out "Pig!" or "Fool!" The atmosphere was tense and volatile inside the church, until finally the heckling got to be too much for the politician. He needed someone to blame, a scapegoat or target for the crowd, which was quickly threatening to turn into a mob. So he placed the blame squarely on the people most immediately identified with the provincial government: the parks officials, including Dave Bishop and Kim Hollings.

"If the province won't act," said the mayor, working himself into a lather, "then we should get Ottawa to send in more men. This is like mad cow disease. Tourists won't come here if they feel they're in danger."

Dave attempted to defend his department, but he was shouted down. The mayor had diverted the mob anger upon a new target, and he was not about to place himself again in the bull's eye.

In his hand was a letter to the editor published in *The Northern Examiner.* He began to read an excerpt, and the hecklers went silent. The letter started with a litany of complaints about the recent bear attacks. The author of the letter, a retired naval officer from New Hampshire, listed reports of tour cancellations from the provincial and local tourist offices. The headline of the letter read: BEARS TURNED ME OFF GROS MORNE, AND I WILL NEVER VISIT AGAIN.

"Dear Editor," the mayor recited, "as a tourist visiting your beautiful island for the first time, I was deeply disappointed by the situation with the Gros Morne bears and the officials who ought to be watching them. I began hearing of bear attacks the moment my wife and I got off the ferry at Port aux Basques. As we travelled the Trans-Canada Highway to Deer Lake and up the Viking Trail to Gros Morne National Park, we often stopped along the way. At Lomond River campsite we saw scavenging or skid row bears, panhandlers and hostile bears. A young boy was attacked by a panhandler near the public toilets at one campsite we visited. The bears made us so nervous that we decided to return home.

"The lack of action by the park and the government makes it clear that you don't want us to visit you. And I thought Americans and Canadians ought to be friends as well as neighbours. Because of the situation in Newfoundland, THIS YANK AIN'T COMING BACK. Richard 'Rich' Richards of Concord, New Hampshire."

The crowd turned on Dave Bishop, demanding answers. He didn't have any.

The next day, the bear attacks finally made national and international news. The presence of victims so close to the Hodden Complex, a popular youth spot, left officials no other choice but to close it. That same day, the province announced it was launching a search-and-destroy action against bears within twenty miles of the complex. No bears were found in the following two weeks, however, and the complex was reopened.

Mail arrived at the station for Dave soon after the national publicity had subsided. A new report on samples arrived from St. John's. The results confirmed what Dave Bishop had suspected all along. The scat had human flesh in it. Upon learning the news, he called Kim Hollings to tell her and to find out if she had heard of any missing persons since April.

Kim informed him that the police were on the lookout for one missing person, a sixteen-year-old male student from Deer Lake. The youth had started out walking to school one morning, but he never made it there. The police had treated the case as a runaway because the boy had talked to his friends at school about going to the mainland. No consideration had been given to bears at the time because they were thought to be in their dens. Since then the boy's parents had heard that he was spotted around the War Memorial in St. John's, dealing dope, begging on the streets and sporting a pink mohawk haircut. The matter was investigated, but none of the youths questioned had seen the boy, and because the sighting was only hearsay, the police had soon given up.

The boy didn't seem to Dave a likely bear-attack victim while reports were still coming in that he was alive. He asked Kim if there had been any other missing persons.

"Only three coastal fishermen several months ago," she said. "We didn't find their bodies. That happened somewhere between Corner Brook and the park."

"Well," said Dave, "we've collected stool samples from bears out that way with human flesh in it."

"That would explain a lot, wouldn't it, Dave?"

"With the way things are going," he said, "that's about the only answer I can come up with."

Armed now with what he believed was a strong lead from the Royal Canadian Mounted Police, Dave felt he could explain the human flesh found in the bear scat. The map of the park on the wall caught his eye as he hung up the phone.

"The farthest sample is eighty miles from the coast," he said to himself. "That's a mighty long way for a bear to travel at that time of year. They're highly territorial, and sows don't travel more than twenty miles from territory they've marked. Boars, maybe forty. Maybe during mating season in May a long migration could be possible, but eighty miles? That's still a long way."

That afternoon, as he was trying to make sense of the conflict between the sample and what he knew of bear migrations, Kim's voice came from the doorway.

"What's up?"

She had removed her last bandage. Her arm and leg had almost fully healed, with just a few telltale blemishes remaining. Dave thought she might need to have plastic surgery to completely remove the claw marks from her arm. At least she was no longer hobbling.

"Just the person I wanted to see," said Dave. "Come over and look at this map. The three men who drowned off the coast were near the lower park line, I guess, early spring. Could you have some men do a check of the beaches for about ten miles either side of the boundary?"

"Sure, but what are we looking for?"

"Get them to look for anything that might have washed ashore in the last month or so. It could be a hat, a glove, boots, anything that might help us."

Kim shook her head.

"What's wrong? You look kind of confused."

"I am," she said. "The fishermen went missing a couple of months ago."

"You're right, but the bodies would decompose slowly in the cold weather of March and April."

"Yes, but I was talking to the police, and I asked about the three fishermen. They think that their bodies may have washed ashore after the search for them ended and the insects and birds got the carcasses. There would not have been enough left of them by now to attract bears."

The phone rang. It was still more bad news for Dave.

"One of Alex's crew has been attacked," he said, turning to Kim.

The caller reported to Dave that he was about four miles away from the office. The injured man was badly mauled, but there was a hospital chopper from Corner Brook on the way to them.

"I'm leaving now," Dave replied.

He and Kim drove into the clearing left by the loggers just as the medical chopper landed. Dave didn't think the man had much chance of pulling through. He had lost a lot of blood and looked ghostly pale.

"The bear was a blur," Alex said. "He was on him in just a matter of seconds, flying twenty-five feet at him.

"It ran straight at him and knocked him down, then bit into his shoulder; it was close to the neck but didn't hit his jugular. It ripped open his belly with just one swipe! God, I hope I never have to see that again. We fired two shots into the animal, and it ran into the brush at the edge of the clearing. We've been hearing a moan coming from there."

"How long ago was it shot?" Dave asked.

"About thirty minutes."

"We'll have to take a look," said Kim.

An officer had a beagle with him, and the animal was clearly agitated, pulling at the leash, struggling to take off in the direction of the bear's escape path.

"Come on, boy," the officer said to the dog, dragging it to the edge of the clearing. Along the way, there were signs of blood on the ground and low bushes.

"Let's find that bear," Dave said grimly.

The dog worked the track, sniffing and waving its head from side to side. They soon came upon more blood on the ground.

"That bear is done, I'm sure of it," Kim said.

Deeper in the woods, in heavy timber on open mossy slopes, the beagle made a low growl and led them up a moose trail. As it rounded a tree, they ran into the bear, lying still, facing them. It appeared to be dead.

"Boy, he's big!" Kim said.

"Let me go in," Dave said.

"No, this is my job, Dave." She turned and addressed the policeman now. "I'll go in. Keep the dog back, will you?"

She pulled out her .44 Ruger, cocked the hammer back and pointed the gun right at the bear's head. She stood about three yards away, about to fire, when its eyes flew open, and it lunged. Three flashes from Kim's barrel ended the bear's life; three rounds found their place inside the animal's skull.

"Stay put, you bastard!" she yelled. Turning around, she said, "It's over, guys. It's dead."

Trembling slightly, she held the pistol grip tight with the barrel pointed down at her side. Kim seemed unaware that she was still holding the gun.

Dave laid a hand on her shoulder.

"You know, you took a chance walking up on a bear," he said. "I once saw a man get clawed up pretty bad doing that. Before I could get a shot away, the bear had him. I'm telling you, they sure know how to play possum."

"I've heard tell of that," sighed Kim. "But this is the first time I've ever seen one do it." She holstered her pistol.

"We need this big guy out of here for analysis," said Dave.

"I'll call the park chopper," said Kim.

"By the way," one of the officers asked, "would anyone have a cigarette?"

A smoke after a bear kill was an old hunting ritual.

"Save it for later," Dave muttered.

10

On the Trail

The chopper dropped the bear off at Wildlife's Deer Lake office. When he returned from checking on the troops working the beaches, it was past seven o'clock, and Dave felt it was time for him to get something to eat. But when he was thinking over his choices, he found he had little appetite for any of the meals that came to mind. He decided to have a beer and leftover pizza.

At eight o'clock Kim turned up with a report about what had been collected. She found him in his lab with the bear spread out on a blue tarpaulin, writing in his notebook.

"You're working late. You must be enjoying this."

The crews had found no bodies, she said, but what they had found they bagged and left at her headquarters for them to check in the morning.

"That's great," Dave said. "Unless we can find something in these bears, we may never know what's happening. I don't even know where to start. Maybe our tests will shed some light on this tomorrow and we'll have something useful to go on."

He looked at the bear's teeth. "What a trophy!" he said. "You should be happy with it. He's not that old, maybe twelve or thirteen. Now all you need is a tooth, a piece of muscle from his hind leg, some stomach samples. With those items, and his measurements here," he said, passing her a sheet, "you can tell his age for sure. It's one of our tags on his ear. I removed it to identify him."

"He's starting to smell," said Kim, wrinkling her nose.

"Yes, we'd better get it out of here tomorrow."

"The fellow who was attacked had a report he was intending to give us," she said. "I found it at my office in an envelope. Did you know that there were only a few samples with bones in the flesh? Others didn't. It seems like someone may be feeding bears muscle and organs removed from bodies."

"That's it," Dave said.

"What!"

"Well," Dave explained, "bears will eat some of the bones from their kill, usually the ribs, arms and legs. If the flesh in their scat has no bones, it's not from a kill."

"I guess someone could be feeding human flesh to them," Kim interjected. "But why remove the bone?"

"That I don't know."

"But who? How? This is such a small place, and everyone knows everyone else. How could they get away with it?"

"We'll have to investigate," said Dave. "But we may have to report that the bears could be feeding on human flesh from somewhere: lab tissue, bio-waste from a hospital or morgue. They're developing a liking for it."

"Abortions are up," Kim said. "You think unauthorized disposal of fetuses could be the source?"

"It may not be one source. We simply don't know enough to say just yet.," Dave said. "But it's probably a safe bet that the bears have turned to humans for food as a result of foul play. Right now we're only guessing, and we should say nothing public about it until we know for sure. I'll brief Alex, but beyond that, we need to keep a lid on it."

Kim helped Dave drag the bear into a walk-in refrigerator.

"I'll have the guys dispose of him tomorrow," she said.

"We meet tomorrow afternoon with a few hunters," said Dave.

"Hunters?"

"Yes. We need to explain the rules when they enter the park."

"And make sure they report all bear sightings," she added.

At the entrance to the park, Dave and Kim met Rick Preston and his two hunting buddies, Ted Schultz and Don Beckman. Each was wearing hiking boots, jeans, a thick woollen shirt, a bright orange hunting vest, a backpack and a baseball cap. Each of them carried a shotgun.

"Why don't we draw match lots?" asked Rick.

"Great," said Beckman. "We'll draw. Whoever gets the shortest match will take the bottomland." He broke three wooden matches from a box he was carrying. Rick and Schultz each pulled one.

"Hah," Rick said, holding up the short match. "I got it."

Schultz turned to Dave. "I've been wondering about those boys who were attacked downtown," he said. "Why are the bears going out of their way to attack people?"

"It could be a couple of things," said Dave. "We know people have been feeding the bears, despite our repeated warnings. The feeding has been going on a long time."

"If people are stupid enough to still feed bears, what can you do?" Preston said. "They almost deserve what they get."

Dave observed Rick in the dim light of early evening. His hair was thinning and he had a ruddy complexion, the face of a drinker and a smoker. He wore a large silver buckle on his belt in the shape of a bear.

Rick took a deep breath of evening air. "I love that smell," he said. "No city smog."

Schultz, in contrast, seemed a more reticent kind of guy, balding and bespectacled. He was shorter than Kim, thinner and frailer-looking than the others. Beckman was a round-bodied man, soft at the edges, with brown hair and sideburns. He had a pinkish complexion, and his large nose had the deep pores typical of rosacea.

"Now, gents," said Dave. "You know what this is about. Two of you will go to your sites with Ranger Hollings. I will accompany Mr. Preston to his site. We'll split up where the river turns south. Remember to note anything unusual on the trails. We'll remove any bears you take and return them after our analysis."

"The bounty still two hundred dollars?" asked the businessman.

"Yep," said Kim.

"Who cares?" said Rick.

"This is fun," Schultz put in. "We usually have to pay big bucks to do this."

Ten minutes later, they clambered to the Humber River point from where they would head toward their respective sites with their sturno cans and honey to lure the bears in. Their feet sank in the mossy forest floor and crunched pine cones and twigs under the deepening skies as they climbed a grassy bluff on the riverbank. They entered along a path that stretched a few hundred yards into thick clumps of poplars and spruces near the water. Below on the trail, away from the water, was a long ditch. They groped through the leaves of saplings and alders growing into the path. Rick led the way, puffing up ahead, followed by Dave, Kim and the others.

Rick stopped suddenly and held up his hand. He pointed to a leafy maple about forty feet up the trail. Against the darkening heavens, the others saw a large black object. Rick put his gun to his shoulder and pulled the trigger. The smoke cleared to reveal that the dark form had backed off the trail.

"I'll get him," he said, taking aim again. A flash erupted from his shotgun, followed by a loud bang.

A moan came from the black shape, and it thudded to the ground.

"Good shot, Rick," said Schultz.

"It doesn't get any better than this," Beckman added.

"Take it easy," said Dave. "The most dangerous time to approach a bear is after you've shot it."

He and Kim had drawn their pistols. The others stepped cautiously ahead of them to the fallen animal, which was lying twenty yards away from the tree where Rick had first seen it. The men held their rifles on the animal.

"Well," said Schultz, walking closer to the animal. "Some bear, Rick."

Beckman just chuckled.

Dave and Kim came upon the men peering at the fallen beast. Rick was scratching his chin. "I could have sworn," he said. "I'll be damned."

"What is it?" Dave asked.

"A moose," said Schultz, laughing. "A one-and-a-half-year-old cow I'd say."

"You stupid bastard!" Dave exclaimed.

"What happened?" Kim asked.

Dave stormed away, taking his hat off and slapping it against his leg.

"That idiot shot a moose!" he called back.

Kim shook her head in disgust.

Continuing along, they soon came to the turn in the river where the trail branched. They divided into two groups and travelled up a narrow valley into the foothills toward a fjord. Dave instructed everyone to return in an hour to the park entrance.

Dave and Rick headed toward the hills, into a canopy of tall alders. Within fifteen minutes, they were at their destination and set up the honey burn.

"What is your theory on the attacks?" Rick asked.

"As I said earlier," Dave said, "we have to take them all until the attacks stop."

"When will that be?"

"Quiet," Dave whispered. A slight rustling sound came from the trees beyond. They waited for darkness, but they heard nothing else. Dave returned his pistol to his holster.

"Must have been a scavenger," said Rick.

"It's time to head back, anyway. Let's take a look."

Flashing the light on the ground for scat, Dave found a fresh set of boot prints, but no sign of a bear.

"Nothing but us or some other hunters here," he said.

At nine o'clock the next morning, they met a grim-faced policeman at the park entrance.

"One of our guards was found this morning," he said. "He'd been mauled to death."

The victim had been found at dawn, the policeman explained, and the body was partially dismembered. The police had conducted a search and spotted a bear on the old logging road, half a mile from the farmhouse where the previous attack had occurred. The police search team had fired a few shots at the animal, but were unable to destroy it before it ran into the tuckamore.

"The stuff it ran into," the policeman said, "was so thick we had no choice but to crawl. It was a mess of alder and hardwood underbrush. Don't know how the bear made it through. It's up to eight feet tall, but bear and moose get through that stuff all the time, I know."

They had cornered another bear an hour later with dogs, he continued, and shot it dead. A few miles farther up the road, they found the remains of the guard. The bear had broken the man's neck, torn flesh from his neck down and consumed some of his thigh. Blowflies were all over the carcass when the police got to it.

"Thank God he was dead before the bear started on him," the officer said. "It must have run with the body, though the animal wasn't that large, maybe one hundred and fifty pounds. And the victim weighed over two hundred pounds."

"The bear was strong enough," said Dave. "The man could have weighed three hundred pounds, and a bear a hundred and fifty pounds lighter would have carried him a few miles without resting, no problem."

"At a gallop," added Kim. "A good gallop."

That afternoon, while Kim and Dave were searching for samples and trapped bears, Jack Crandall pulled up to the park entrance. The policeman from Deer Lake recognized him.

"You can't go in right now, Jack," he said. "The park's closed for the day. Police investigation."

"I see that," said Jack. "I was just going to pick up a few things I had stashed down the road near one of my old sites. It's only about ten miles from here; I'll be in and out in half an hour."

"No," said the policeman. "Not today."

Jack turned his truck around and waved to the policeman. Just then, Dave and Kim appeared at the edge of the forest. By the time they reached the police guard, Jack's truck was just a speck on the highway.

11

The Foil

Jack found Starlight as fast-growing and as inquisitive as Calvin had been. That evening, the young bear pushed open Jack's verandah door, which had been left unlocked. Most bears are hungry all the time, and even a yearling would not hesitate to test a door. Earlier that afternoon, Jack had weighed the bear on a pair of large butcher scales he kept near the shed; the bear's weight, one hundred and eighty pounds, startled him, for most bears Starlight's age were thirty pounds lighter.

The bear scouted Jack's modestly furnished seating area. The windows of the cottage served to frame a quarter-acre of neglected, fallow ground, and a run-down flower garden. The property didn't have the expanse of the lodge, and between Jack's work at the funeral home and Dorothy's physical infirmities, they hadn't had the time and energy to fix up the place. An electrified wire fence to discourage hungry thieves like Starlight protected the property. The bear had felt the jolt of current from the fence several times, and he had quickly learned to avoid the few beds of vegetables Jack managed to set out. But the door to the house presented no obstacle, and the smells wafting out were an invitation no healthy young bear could refuse.

Part of the allure was man-made. Jack and his wife often had morning coffee and doughnuts in the kitchen, and in the evenings they sometimes sat quietly together behind the screened windows, well protected from mosquitoes. The room was furnished with two rockers, a maple wood coffee table, a white chaise lounge and leftover furniture from Jack's hunting lodge. On the wall were reproductions of the *Lion Hunt* by E. Delacroix and *On the Move* by A. Kiss.

Starlight was standing and falling on all fours, raising himself back on his hind legs and having a fine old time. Softly he stepped on padded feet, like some very large black pillow. The wood floor of the verandah was strewn with hemp throw rugs that cushioned his steps. When a bear and people were in the same neck of the woods, the animal could as well have been walking on air, unless it wanted to be heard. On the other hand, a bear had a range of hearing far greater than any human, and in the wild, what it could not hear or see, it sensed through smell.

Starlight did not have to see yesterday's crumbs on the verandah floor. He stuck his snout under the furniture and started licking up morsels hidden from sight. As Starlight pushed and tilted the furniture, he relished the cornucopia of minute human leftovers—tiny, plentiful, tasty. He was as happy as if he had found ants under a log.

But bears are unable to retract their claws, and every once in a while, Starlight made a light *tat-tat* sound, his claws scratching against exposed parts of the hardwood floor.

Dorothy happened that very moment to be walking across the hall between the kitchen and the downstairs bathroom. She passed the door in the hallway when she heard what she thought to be movement and scratches against the floor. She glanced through the door window out onto the verandah, stopped and looked again, this time more carefully.

"Jack!" she cried in disbelief. "Jack! The bear's on the verandah!"

Jack was dozing in front of his television and oblivious to the fact that the six o'clock news had ended. He had fallen asleep somewhere between the local news and the weather forecast. *Oh boy,* he thought, waking to Dorothy's voice, *what now?* He assumed right away that she had left the hall door unlocked, though the odds were much greater that he had committed the oversight himself. A crisis worth waking him for? It was only Starlight on the verandah, standing on his hind legs and looking back at the two of them through a window.

Jack stepped onto the verandah and closed the door behind him. The bear's beady black eyes gazed steadily at him. The large beast went down on all fours and became very still, obstinate and uncertain. Tentatively, the bear began sniffing him. Then he gave way, turning around and running in full retreat. When Starlight left the steps, he pranced hurriedly to the shed. Finding the shed door closed, the bear waited patiently. When Jack reached the shed door and opened it, Starlight dashed inside.

In the back room of the shed was a hollowed-out space that Jack had made for Starlight's den. The slight indentation was in a corner, and nearby were freshly cut branches of saplings and a large pail of water. On the shed floor lay part of a moose hindquarter. The bear leapt on the meat, tearing the flesh with his teeth, crunching the bones and greedily swallowing the marrow.

Starlite ate all the time, wholly in character for bears; indeed, he never went hungry for more than an hour. Mice, squirrels and shrews all but disappeared near the barn once the bear settled there. His claws and fangs were fully capable of taking down a young moose. Chiefly, however, he foraged on grass, roots, grubs and herbs, but his favourite foods were honey and doughnuts. To this fare were sometimes added balls of caribou meat and moose hamburger as a late evening treat.

After Starlight fed on the moose, he left for his regular nocturnal forage in the nearby fields. Once the animal was out of the barn, Jack headed back to the crematorium to finish cleaning the burner. He would scrape out the residue left in the retort, for there were always minute bone fragments of the last corpse among the ashes. The stiff metal bristles of his rake would catch the bone chips and shards and he would sweep them into a metal pan at the bottom of the grill. The bone chips he fed into the industrial-size grinder, pulverizing them into a fine grit. Jack would then sweep the oven again and vacuum out from the cracks in the brick surface the remaining particles and ashes. While cleaning the retort for the next cremation, he took care not to commingle the cremains.

Jack's absence in the evenings so piqued Dorothy's curiosity that she decided to ask him what he was doing so late at night. She had gotten over her initial shock at seeing the bear on the verandah and had come out to the shed to see her husband off.

"I have to finish a job," he explained. "That way I won't have to catch up tomorrow."

The next evening Dorothy became even more curious when Jack began to pack his sleeping bag and a large thermos of coffee to take with him.

"Are you spending the night at the funeral home?"

"I think I might have to," Jack said. "Norm said bodies are piling up. I'll call you later to let you know."

"What about the bear?"

"He'll be fine. I'll leave the door to the shed unlocked so he can get in and out. Don't worry about Starlight; he'll be fine. Why don't you go to bed?"

"Okay," Dorothy said. "As long as I don't have to do anything for him."

"I'll call you if I stay over."

"What's all the garlic and pepper for?"

"Someone gave it to me. I thought we might use it later in the fall."

When he was alone, Jack's thoughts turned to Starlight's welfare. What was he going to do with him? Starlight got into a lot of mischief, breaking the chairs, tables, glass jars and dishes stored in the shed, even if he showed no signs of menace to either Jack or his wife. Starlight appeared on his way to becoming a transient part of his life, showing more mischief than obedience. Aside from the time Jack commanded Starlight to play with him, the bear mostly had a mind of his own; often he chose to abandon his human provider in order to follow a scent or sound known only to himself. During such lapses of attention, he would ignore Jack's calls and would not even respond to bribes, unless they were instantly forthcoming and supplied long enough for him to forget whatever had caught his eye.

Jack also knew that Starlight had already established his territory around the cottage and shed. Woe to any intruding fox, coyote or other wild predators that ventured into the boundary of Starlight's kingdom while he was in residence. Caribou and moose gave the place a wide berth, as Starlight maintained a vigilance over his realm from a perch sixty feet up a tall maple, grunting, woofing and racing down to confront and chase any intruder from the forest. The bear was safe on Jack's land from all of the bounty hunters in the neighbourhood; his modest cottage lay several miles from the highway and some twenty-five miles from the park. The property nestled beyond the mountains east of the southern tip of the park. Two centuries earlier, it would have been a royal land grant or homestead for an intrepid pioneer. Without any immediate neighbours, the house and shed made a lonely sight.

Since the outbreak of the bear attacks, Jack had been feeling uneasy. For the last three weeks, his regrets had only grown with news of the investigation. With all the reports he had read about and seen on television, he knew it was possible Starlight would be killed in the cropping. Jack also began to feel that someone might suspect him of tampering with the bears.

He had come to a decision, to use his experience to stop the rash of attacks in Gros Morne Park. His plan was simple: he would scatter the deterrent around the eastern end of the park. Strong doses of condiments added to human remains would kill the bears' desire to hunt down and devour tourists and residents.

At five o'clock the next morning, Jack looked out the window of the crematorium. Rain was falling lightly. His boss would not be there until nine or ten.

He gathered together body parts and put them in the large grinder next to the sink. These remains were practically unindentifiable as human, the mangled leftovers from head-on collisions and other brutal, tragic accidents. He flicked the electric switch and began taking the ground meat from the grinder and placing it on the table he used for washing corpses.

When Jack struck on his plan to dissuade bears of their fondness for human prey, he remembered an incident from a few years back. Dorothy had been on the Tablelands and stumbled on a bizarre flower, nearly impossible to spot among the bare, moonlike rubble of peridotite. This was an ancient rock solidified from the mantle of the earth, now thrust upon the surface by tectonic forces of nature. In the Tableland soil, Dorothy had found a small, dirt-brown flower, its leaves only half an inch long. The petals were more exotic than pretty. In colour and pattern, they mimicked the nutrient-deficient coarse soil, grudgingly freed from the alien-looking rock under the stresses of heat and cold, and the actions of air and water.

Jack remembered that the leaves—or petals—made his old beagle sick. Dorothy had placed her unusual nosegay in a small vase on the patio table, and dried leaves and petals had blown into the dog's food bowl. This beagle wasn't a fussy eater, and a few foreign objects in its bowl was no excuse to go hungry. A few petals remained scattered about the dog's dish; others stuck to the remaining food, the plant's camouflage naturally blending with the colour and texture of the dog meal. He had found King cowering under the patio deck, lethargic, and whimpering, his belly distended with intestinal gas. The discomfort eased up in a few hours, and King lived another year before passing on to doggy heaven.

He picked up a generous handful of garlic and pepper mix, wrapped it tightly in plastic wrap and encased this concoction inside a ball of ground meat. He repeated the procedure again and again, and when he had enough, he added a few leaves and petals of this plant to each garlic and pepper bait. The new ingredients might not be lethal, but they might intensify the bears' gastric distress.

The bears that he feared had developed a taste for human flesh would find and eat the meatballs and develop a bad case of indigestion. Very soon the bears would learn to avoid human flesh, attacks in Gros Morne would end, and no one but Jack would ever know the truth.

He cleaned the grinder and washed down the metal table where he had prepared the bait. When he was done, he went to the freezer to move a body to the crematorium furnace.

Jack said to himself, "How in hell does he get so many bodies? We're getting one or two every day. Old gizzards and biddies."

He removed an elderly soul from the freezer shelf, placed him on a gurney and rolled it over to the furnace. He removed the name tag from the corpse's foot and placed it beside a large can marked for the ashes. He then put on his asbestos-lined apron, a sheet that covered his shoulders. After donning his asbestos gloves and covering his face and head with a protective mask, Jack opened the furnace door, the familiar blast of hot air hitting him solidly. He shoved the body into the retort, locked the door, and adjusted the temperature of the gas oven to 1500°F. Noticing the sunlight pouring into the room, Jack checked his watch again and went to work sweeping and washing the floor. The gas jets hummed and heat radiated upward into the room.

When he was done, he cleaned the retort and put the ashes in an urn. He placed the urn in Norm's office with a note saying he would cremate the other bodies tomorrow.

A few hours later, he turned off the Viking Trail onto a network of dirt roads around the perimeter of the park. He travelled to eight different sites over the next few hours. Knowing that each site was well travelled by bears, he stopped at each one and selected a spot where he could bury the meat he had laced. First he emptied buckets of garlic-and-pepper portions into the hole he dug. Then he laid atop each pile a couple of pieces of the fresh, untainted meat. After baiting the eight sites, he returned to his truck and drove home.

During the bear's first molt in June, Jack had rubbed fur all over the rough wood of the shed walls; his favourite maple had gobs of fur stuck to its trunk. Some days Dorothy would walk by the shed and give the molt-covered walls a critical look. Then she would hear the bear snoring softly inside and think better of cleaning up. At other times, she would hear the rapid tapping of its claws when he would rise to greet her or Jack at the shed's door. Despite his ungainly, flat-footed gait, Starlight's pads often enabled him to sneak up on her outside the house. She would look up from what she was doing, startled by the bear sitting calmly beside her. There was nothing wrong with her hearing—

she had just not heard it approach her. The bear still made her uneasy, but she didn't have the strength to argue with Jack.

Jack came home and woke her up. He decided to eat brunch with her and have a nap before going to work in the afternoon.

"What are you going to do with him?" Dorothy asked between sips of tea. "We can't keep a bear here."

"He's going to go off on his own in a year," said Jack. "He'll take a fancy to a sow next year and be gone. Starlight isn't bothering anybody right now. He can stay for a while."

"Bears can't live with people. You always said that."

"It's true."

"They're wild," Dorothy said. "Not like a dog."

"They're the most wild," Jack agreed. "The most alive when they're wild, the most alive when they're free, and no bear's gonna be cooped up for long, you better believe that."

"I think Calvin would have made it a pet."

At the mention of his late son, Jack fell into silence. Dorothy's eyes glistened. The couple said nothing further as Jack rose from the table to get another cup of coffee.

The next day, when Jack returned home from work, his supper was waiting for him on the stove. Dorothy was watching television in the living room. After he had showered and changed his clothes, he ate his meal, then took a run into town for a can of coffee.

"Boy, there are a lot of police around," he said to Dorothy when he returned home. "You would think there was a crime wave going on."

"They're on the news every night," said Dorothy.

"Bears move more at night than they do in the daytime."

"Do you think they can stop them from killing people, Jack?"

"I don't know," he said, "but in time the park staff might figure things out."

PART III

12

The Hunter and the Hunted

Norm Cotten checked in at the funeral home at noon the next day. Jack was troubled and it showed on his face.

"You been feeling okay, Jack?" Norm said.

"Yes, sure."

"I was only wondering whether you needed more time off," Norm said. He and Jack presented a stark contrast in work clothes, the former in a black suit and wire-rimmed glasses, the latter in jeans and woollen grey shirt.

"Would you like some time off?"

"Sure, but can I ask why?" Jack said.

"Well," said the mortician, "I was thinking you might like some time with your wife."

"Well, I also need to work, you know."

Norm shook his balding head, rubbing his hands together. "I have another fellow I'd like to take on to help you," he said. "We're short-handed since Mark passed away. I still don't know what happened to him."

"It was a coronary," said Jack. "It was in the report."

"But he was so young," said the mortician, "so strong and healthy."

He shook his head, vigorously this time. Then he looked Jack straight in the eyes.

"You know," he said in a level tone. "I received a call from the park ranger's office asking whether we had any missing or mutilated corpses. They asked to come here and look around if I would permit it. I don't see any problem with that. But I thought it would be better for you that you weren't here when they come. I'm only trying to help you, you know."

"Everybody knows what happened to me," Jack said. "I have no problem with the park anymore."

"Well," Norm persisted, "I'm only trying to help."

"I'll be fine."

Norm's expression was irritated now.

"Well," he said with a shrug. "I won't need you here for the next few days. When you clean up, leave the key to the morgue in my office. I'll see you next week."

He turned and left the room before Jack could reply.

"Oh," Jack said. "What an ass." But he realized there was no choice. The investigations were getting too close for comfort.

"Thanks, Norm," he said, still staring at the door. "I'll really appreciate my vacation."

Dorothy was on the lawn when Jack pulled into the driveway. She was dripping sweat from her exertions, struggling with garden shears and trying hard not to accept the limitations caused by her stroke. Jack offered to finish the job for her, and she gladly accepted, offering him a beer first. As he sipped his beer and Dorothy a cup of tea, Jack tried to make small talk, but Dorothy was too weary.

"I think I'll take a nap," she said.

Jack told her he would cut wood for a couple of hours after he mowed the lawn. He was lying to her, a deception he knew couldn't be helped.

When he had finished mowing, he got in his truck and sped off down the highway.

While he was gone, Dorothy rose from her nap, thinking she would go out and clean up the yard. She cooked some homemade pork and beans to have with Jack for their supper that evening, and she baked some biscuits to go with it. The leftovers would be good for a couple of meals.

Dorothy thought about Starlight. Oh, what to do about him? He was such a rough, dirty creature! She recalled that Jack had been taking things out of the shed. She had not been in there for some time, and now, out of idle curiosity, she had an urge to find out what in the world he had been doing in there. The bear, she knew, would already be gone; it was late in the afternoon, and Starlight would be in the woods somewhere foraging for berries and honey.

She went into the shed and found it dark, and so smelly she sneezed. Starlight was there! Her sneeze had startled him. He sat on his haunches and stared at her as though he was as surprised to see her as she was to see him. The bear itself was part of the awful stench in the shed; the odour so sickened her that she turned to leave.

The bear followed her all the way back and onto the verandah.

"Get away," Dorothy said, slamming the door in the bear's face.

Starlight leaned into the door and when it did not give immediately, he scratched at it and began tearing off wallboards along the clapboard siding as if they were tissue paper. He put his paws flat against the screens of the windows and ripped them. He clawed the edges of the windowpanes until the wooden frames loosened, then smashed the window to make a big enough hole to wedge through.

"Go, Starlight!" Dorothy shouted. "Get away from there!"

But Starlight's mind was made up. He fixed her with a steady glare. She started shrieking, and he lifted his forepaw and demolished what was left of the windowpanes. Starlight leapt through the opening and landed on the floor. Dorothy, nearly hysterical, raced down the hall and closed the kitchen door behind her. No sooner was she behind the door than Starlight pounded it until it too gave way. He stalked across the linoleum floor, his head thrust forward and swaying. He caught Dorothy's dress in his teeth and sat down hard, pulling her toward him.

"Get away from me! Let me go!"

Her protests did not sway him. Starlight tightened his grip. The force of his jaws ripped the dress, temporarily freeing her, but his claws quickly snared her again. He let her free of his grasp for a few seconds, only to push his snout into her chest or poke her under her arms, turning and tossing her about the floor. The woman was scratched and breathing hard, her face flushed in panic. She attempted to crawl away, but each time she tried, the bear played with her as a cat would a cornered mouse.

Dorothy's heart throbbed painfully in her chest—she needed her heart medication. The bear continued his deadly play, his vigilance and energy never slacking. Dorothy moved more feebly each time Starlight grabbed her with his paws. The bear would lick her, get up and walk around, and as soon as she moved, he would return in a flash, toss her to the floor, and plant a paw on her chest. Part of his game was pretending to ignore her, only to seize her as soon as she attempted to escape. Not a movement was lost on him. Every time she tried to get up, he would torment her.

Dorothy's only hope at this desperate moment was outside help. Jack might return to rescue her, or if somehow she could reach the telephone to call the police, she might stand a chance. She waited quietly for the bear to leave her, hoping he would become hungry and start looking for food outside. He didn't seem to want her for that reason. As soon as he abandoned playing with her, she decided, she had to make a dash to her telephone on the wall and dial for emergency help.

Miraculously, the bear paused and moved away. Now Dorothy played dead and waited for him to leave the house. Starlight moved to the doorway and licked at the floor. Dorothy began to gasp for air, after holding her breath for as long as she could. She rose to take a step for the telephone and was halfway there when the bear, as game as ever, struck her with his right paw. She saw bright cascades of rockets as her head struck the kitchen counter. The room blurred as she lay on her back on the floor. The bear began to lick blood from her fresh wound. He snorted, stepped on her chest and rested there on top of her, scrutinizing her face for a response.

In a few minutes, Dorothy lay very still. The bear kept pressing down hard, and when she did not respond, he licked her face and sniffed at her. Seeing that the game was over and won, Starlight made his way out of the kitchen and down the hall to the verandah. He stopped on the lawn to relieve his bowels and bladder. When he was finished, he headed for a stream running off the nearby Humber River, in search of the food he relished most—berries, roots and honey.

When Jack found his wife on the kitchen floor, he knew instantly what had happened. It was not so much the state of the kitchen or the blood on her face, but the look in her eyes. Her eyes were glazed and open wide, in the final, asphyxiated recognition of her demise. Her arms were cold, a familiar clammy cold to him, and he knew she was gone.

Now he had lost his closest and dearest, and again he felt tears in his eyes. Not the tears of grief, but of the same old hatred and rage. The chain of events that had brought the bear into his life had led to Dorothy's death. And the people responsible for her death were the objects of his bitterness.

In a moment he was loose and limber, the invisible blows of his losses falling without pain. Calvin and now Dorothy, the loss of the ones he loved. But he would not grieve for them. He wouldn't cry out in pain. He would take it; he would embrace the loss, the sooner to end the sharp current that was trying to hurt him so he would want to mourn and to weep. No, he would not mourn, but he could not stop himself from feeling the urge for revenge.

The bear was his only friend now. For all Jack knew, he was soon to lose his only job. *So this is how life ends*, he thought bitterly, *lonely, afraid, broke, filled with fear and trembling and sickness.*

He would have to clean and dress Dorothy, leave the kitchen as it was, and call the police. He dreaded the call, but it had to be done.

There was no way Jack could hide that this had been a bear attack, nor would he attempt to do so. But no one needed to know about Starlight. He would give a description of a bear, a sow so unlike Starlight that everyone would be looking for another animal. All the same, he knew that Starlight's days were probably numbered. The hunters were destroying every bear they came across and Jack felt that he had to protect him as best he could.

He sat up all night, and at dawn, he went outside to a cool, damp day. The icebergs on the east side of the island had drawn close to shore. Winds would blow off them and the temperature on the island would drop to as low as thirty degrees overnight, producing snow flurries even in June. When the wind blew the icebergs away from the shore, the weather warmed once again.

This sudden shift in temperature was part of the magic of Newfoundland.

There was no way of further delaying the inevitable. He picked up the phone and called the police to report a bear attack. Next he called Dorothy's sister and told her the sad news.

At the funeral home, Norm looked uncomfortable in Jack's presence. He attempted to lay a hand on Jack's shoulder in a gesture of friendship and sympathy, but Jack was having none of it. Jack felt Norm was unreasonable by insisting that he take a week off work, further insulting him by hiring another man to conduct funerals and cremations. He stormed out of Norm's office.

He greeted friends and relatives throughout the visitation period, which he kept as brief as possible. In a bitter, ironic twist, Jack had to arrange to have his wife cremated at Cotten's Mortuary and Crematorium as an alternative to a more expensive arrangement.

Her sister was okay with cremation. "It's fine," she said. "Dorothy wouldn't want to be a burden on you, Jack."

After a memorial service and cremation, Jack and Dorothy's sister scattered her ashes over a peaceful hill on the Crandalls' old lodge property, which was still abandoned since last year.

Jack had never felt the need to be alone as strongly as he did over the next few days. The police searched his house, and the coroner's report came back to confirm that Dorothy had suffered a heart attack induced by a bear break-in. Dave Bishop, the biologist, had been sympathetic; Kim Hollings, the ranger who had known Calvin, was also kind. One evening shortly after the police had finished investigating Dorothy's death, Jack heard hunters on his property. He knew that Rick Preston was probably among them, back again in

Newfoundland when he heard of the bear cull, and the thought set Jack's blood boiling.

When night fell, he would go into the shed and find Starlight. The bear's face was a portrait of impassivity. He did not approach Jack to beg or to get his attention. It was as though he knew he had done something wrong. But to Jack the bear was not at fault; he had done only what he had been conditioned to do.

After he had fed Starlight, Jack would coax him out of the shed and lead him to the stream, where the bear spent many evenings frolicking.

One day shortly after Dorothy's funeral, Starlight headed for a bank on a hill across from the stream where Jack knew hunters were waiting in stands.

Jack stood passively on the low side of a thicket, wearing a bright luminescent vest. He lowered himself to the ground and observed movement in the brush near the water. Suddenly a man emerged. It was Jack's old nemesis, Rick Preston, holding a shotgun at the ready.

"Man. I thought for a moment I had a bear. Jack, how are you? Sorry to hear about your wife."

Jack ignored the insincere gesture. "What are you doing here?"

Preston reeked of liquor. Jack said nothing as the American pulled out a joint.

"They ought to let you shoot that bear," Rick said as he lit up. "It was your wife. Here." Preston offered Jack his weapon.

Jack stared at the shotgun. He was about to wave Rick away, when he heard a light splash nearby.

"You sure?" he asked Rick.

"Go for it. I'm going to sit and have a toke. I don't need another trophy."

Jack took the offered shotgun and set off toward the stream. He heard a twig snap close to the thicket in front of him. When he spotted Starlight, he raised the shotgun, aiming for his head. The bear sat cooperatively on its hindquarters, waiting for his execution, but Jack stepped back and almost fell into the stream when he stumbled on a branch. He could smell the soporific smoke from Rick wafting through the bushes.

"A bear for a druggie and a killer," Jack muttered.

Before he could lower the shotgun, Rick came stumbling down towards him.

Jack turned away from Starlight.

"Hey," Rick shouted. "Jack, there's a bear behind you! Shoot it!"

Jack turned toward the bear once more and was pleased to see that Starlight had retreated into the woods.

Rick took a long drag of his joint and pointed to the alder. He inhaled deeply and closed his eyes, and behind him Starlight's black shape appeared. In a fraction of a second, the bear closed in and struck the back of the American's neck and back with his powerful paw. There was a sharp crack, and Rick crumpled to the ground. The bear shook him a couple of times, and not getting an immediate response, sat back on his haunches and stared at the still form, ready to pounce on Rick if he made the slightest movement. But Rick did not move. Jack went to him and checked the man's vital signs.

Rick Preston was quite dead.

A feeling of vindication surged through Jack's veins. This was the moment he had yearned for; justice had been served, for Calvin, and now for Dorothy as well. Rick had been responsible, if indirectly, for Dorothy's death by putting in motion the chain of events following Calvin's demise. The law of the wild had given Jack a sense of closure. Everything had come full circle. The hunter had become the hunted and now lay dead.

The bear had hit Rick with enough force to break the spine of a fully grown moose. Jack had seen it before. He had once witnessed a bear run a moose down, cornering it against a cliff, and delivering such a blow with its paw that the entire forest echoed with a terrific crack, like the sound of lightning splitting a tree.

Starlight sat on his haunches, waiting for his reward. Jack took an apple from his coat pocket and threw it to him. The bear devoured the apple, then took off at a sprint to find more plentiful fare.

A few days later, at the ranger station, Dave, Kim and Alex Hagen examined two bears killed the previous night and discussed the death of Rick Preston.

"It looks like he died from a bear attack," Dave said. "He was intoxicated, according to the coroner's report. He probably had no time to fire his shotgun."

"A wild bear normally would have eaten part of him," Alex speculated, "but he only had scratch marks, a broken back and neck, and slight puncture wounds consistent with bear bites."

"It must have been the sow," Kim suggested, "the same one that had attacked Mrs. Crandall. She wasn't eaten either."

Dave examined the stomach of one of the bears on the table. At first, all he detected was grass and tree buds, but when he squeezed the lower intestines, there, in a grassy clump, was some undigested flesh with what appeared to be bone mixed in.

"This, gentlemen, is what a bear's intestines should look like when they've eaten raw meat," he said.

Kim nodded. "Alex, this bear was shot less than two miles from where your man was attacked. The two bears that were spotted last week could easily be from the same lot that crashed the boy scouts' camp."

"Look at this!" Alex exclaimed. He washed something off under a tap, then held up a piece of clear plastic.

"Get the sample from the bear that the taxidermist shot on Saturday," Dave said excitedly. They removed the sample from the fridge and began to look through it. It too contained human flesh. Dave checked it for bone fragments to see if it had been one of the bears that had killed the policeman, but found none.

"Look," said Dave. "This sample has no bone fragments."

"Yes," Kim said. She sneezed. "But what's that smell?"

"It smells like garlic to me," said Dave. He sneezed, and his eyes began to water.

"Pepper there, too," Kim said.

"Let's check the stool from this one," Dave said. When he removed excrement from the dead bear's bowels, he sneezed again.

"You're right. It's black pepper."

"No wonder he hasn't eaten in days," Alex said. "He must have had one severe case of heartburn!"

"I wonder what he could have gotten into?" Dave said.

"Maybe he has Italian blood," said Kim.

"Would you open the door? For God's sake!" Alex protested. "The fumes are so strong, they're reaching us way over here!"

"Let's get this one outside," Dave said. "That's the only way we'll be able to work on it!"

Later that morning, they found two pieces of plastic wrap in another bear's stomach. Inside the wraps were pepper and garlic powder. It had been shot before it's meal worked itself through the digestive system, and the wrap hadn't had time to come loose.

"Garlic for sure," Dave observed. "And this looks like meat blackened in pepper. And what's this? Leaves, and flower petals. That's strange. I've never seen anything like it, in all my years of studying local flora."

The delicate flower petals had survived, since gastric juices hadn't penetrated the wrap.

"We'll have to get this checked out," he said.

The samples would be sent to St. John's to determine if the meat was human. The white powder was indeed garlic, but no one had any idea where the bear could have eaten it, or why he'd even think of eating it. When they finished their autopsy, they went back inside. "No bones either."

"What we have here," Dave said, "are meat-and-bone samples, and meat-and-garlic samples. None of these samples has bone *and* garlic.

"Where do the bears roam?" he asked. "Perhaps the ones in the park have moved out much farther from here. Then there are those that are out seventy to eighty miles. All these bears have returned to their main feeding grounds. And folks, a bear can travel forty miles a day without working up a sweat if he knows where he's going."

"Sounds good," Kim said. "What's your theory on the bear shot by the taxidermist?"

"Don't know if the flesh was human. We should know for sure in a couple of days."

"Well," she said, "if it's human remains, and there's no bones in it, there must be some crazy guy out there removing organs or stripping the meat off bodies and using it for bait."

13

A Clue in the Wild

That afternoon, Dave, Kim and Alex studied a map of Gros Morne park and the western part of Newfoundland. Dave marked those places on the map where the bear attacks had occurred, taking note of the areas where garlic-and-pepper-laced samples had been found. They had spent the day making posters and putting them around the town. Dave had already made phone calls to the few funeral homes in the area, and to the island's organ and tissue labs to inquire about any missing corpses.

"What do you think of conducting a search here?" he asked, pointing to a circled part of the map around the Lomond River near Deer Lake.

"Well, it looks promising," said Alex, "but the flies and mosquitoes are murder right now. It's near impossible to walk through the underbrush."

"The locals can teach you how to walk on top of the trees," Dave said, laughing. "It's the only way to the hills by foot unless you cut a trail." Dave's manner was casual, his tone confident and upbeat.

"Well, Dave, the tuckamore does make my job very difficult when tracking the bears after an attack," said Kim.

"Trapping them is too slow," he said. "And I'm not sure that we will be able to trap the older, smarter ones. If we see a big one, we ought to take it down if it can't be tranquilized. It may help us if we do tests to determine what kind of shape it's in and identify what it's been eating."

"Man," Alex said, peering into a dissected intestine section of a bear, "I don't think this one has eaten anything else in a couple of days."

"We have a preliminary lab report?" asked Dave.

"Yep, but nothing new," Kim said. "We have other samples with flesh covered in garlic and pepper."

Dave took a deep breath. "Where did those other samples come from?"

"Two of them were found out past the Scott farm, and one over here in the park."

"That's forty miles apart," Alex said. "The sample that had bones was from the Big Falls area. This isn't good."

Dave peered at the map.

"These bears are all from different areas," said Kim. "There's no way they could hit the same garlic and pepper, and I can't understand why they'd want to eat it." Turning away from Dave, she addressed Alex directly. "How did we make out with that bear today? Everything normal?"

"Everything seems normal. He sure was a big one. We put his age at twenty-four years."

"Yes, he should break some records," Dave added. "The best thing we can do is keep taking samples from those same areas and see what we find. Maybe we do have a crazy running around here."

"I'm glad to hear that," Kim said, rolling her eyes.

"Find anything there?" Dave asked Alex.

"Yes," his colleague replied, picking up a sample of gut from another bear. "This old stool sample was found near the highway a couple of days ago, but there's also human flesh in it."

"What!" Dave exclaimed. "There hasn't been anyone eaten by a bear in the last few weeks that we know of."

"That's not all. We collected some scat in the park yesterday, and it had human flesh in it, too. The others there just had grass or buds."

Dave shook his head, perplexed.

"Kim and I have been talking to other rangers," Alex continued. "We've been looking at a place in the park where people could have gone missing late last fall or earlier last year. The area is within a ten-mile radius of where we found the samples. We were wondering if there was any way that the bears didn't finish their kill in the upper elevations where it's cool enough to preserve a body, and later found what remained."

"That sounds reasonable," said Dave, "but we really can't tell. I'm sure the lab could tell us if it's a kill from last fall or from this spring."

"Do you really think we have a crazy on our hands, Dave?" Alex asked.

"I wish I knew."

The garlic and pepper, Dave noted, could be very important to solving the attacks and stopping them. He remembered some Newfoundland folklore saying that feeding bears unpalatable additives such as mothballs was a good means of stopping them from eating the moose and caribou, as well as from eating garbage. But how would you get the bear to eat it?

"Of course," he said to himself. "Not *on* their food, but *in* it.

He turned to Kim and Alex. "You wrap the garlic and pepper in plastic wrap and put it inside some ground human flesh, meat without bones made into hamburger. Bears eat the meat, not sensing the garlic and pepper, until the wrap loosens in the stomach and they get sick. They stop eating the flesh. Right?"

"That has to be what's going on!" Kim said excitedly.

"Where are the lab reports on the samples from yesterday?" Dave asked, shuffling through a pile of papers on her desk. He found them and examined them hurriedly. St. John's hadn't been able to visually identify the leaves and flower in the scat samples. They seemed to be from a species not previously collected and classified.

"What about our moose and caribou herds?" said Kim. "They're at record numbers."

"They've been good," Dave replied. "We know the cows and calves survived this past winter."

"What's that got to do with anything?" Alex asked.

"Everything," Dave said. "The bears around here haven't eaten any moose or caribou. We haven't found any in the stool samples we have."

"Get out of here! You're sure?"

"Positive. The herds seem to be staying in good shape around here."

"What about the caribou and moose on the other side of the island?"

"The herds on the rest of the island are declining," Kim said. "Maybe they're all moving into this area. There's not much poaching going on, maybe a dozen or so a year, less than what it was ten to twenty years ago."

"The person feeding bears this stuff is unintentionally benefiting other wildlife," Alex said.

"What about road kills," asked Dave. "Do the bears eat any of them overnight?"

"No," Kim said. "But we do have two or three people stripping meat off the hindquarters before we can get them picked up."

"Do you have any idea who it is?"

She shook her head. "They've been doing it for maybe the past eight years. There really isn't any harm in it, and if someone can use it to put meat on the table to feed their family, who cares? Why all the questions, Dave?"

"I'm thinking that whoever is taking the meat may be saving the island's moose and caribou herds."

"Now, what in the world would make you think that?"

"I'm working on a theory," he said. "I'm thinking that whoever is doing this is taking the meat and lacing it with the spices wrapped in plastic. Then he just drops them where he thinks the bear will find them: lakes, rivers, brooks, logging roads. Probably in berry fields as well."

Kim nodded. "I'll tell head office in St. John's about this."

"You know," Alex said, "they might just laugh at you if you tell them that someone is feeding this stuff to the bears."

"They won't if I tell them that Dave thinks so too."

"There are lots of animals here," said Alex, "plenty for the bears to eat. If only we could get them to leave humans alone."

"He's done that," Dave replied. "We have about eight to ten samples of human flesh in the stools with no bones. We also have some with bones, and three with pepper and garlic in them. Our culprit seems to be trying to turn the bears from humans."

"Exactly," said Kim.

"The bears aren't eating the road kills," Dave continued, "and I think that's why. They will not eat moose or caribou meat again because of the preference for and abundance of defenceless humans."

"We need some way to detect the bears," Alex said, "to see what they are eating when they eat it. If we could see a bear coming upon a body ..."

"We don't have enough people for a thorough bear search," Dave said.

"We know that the moose and caribou show a ten-percent increase over last year," said Kim. "In fact, herd numbers have been rising now for seven years straight. Do you know how we know?"

"You use digital cameras and satellite telemetry."

"That's it."

"You're suggesting wiring the bears?" Alex asked.

"Better," said Kim. "We ought to add digital cameras to our tracking efforts, to see if they have been eating human flesh. Follow them. We ought to see what they see for a few weeks."

"We can record the images by using satellites to transmit signals back to our video monitors," Dave suggested.

"Do you have a budget for that?" his colleague asked.

"We will later today."

"This 'crazy' who you're talking about is a genius," said Kim, pointing to the map. "A real genius."

"And who do you think this person might be?" asked Dave. "Any ideas?"

"No, but I bet you gentlemen will find more samples out there. Someone is trying to discourage the bears from eating people. Who knows at this point? I'm sure we can get emergency funds for the cameras and equipment, though. Let's give it a try."

"This has been a very interesting day, guys," Alex said. "First the garlic-and-pepper evidence, and now a possible suspect."

Late afternoon the next day found Dave and Kim in Gros Morne park, with Pete Humphries, a local dog handler and guide, making up a team. Alex Hagen headed up a second team. Among the equipment laid out on a plastic sheet before them were a digital camera attached to a collar, hypodermic syringes, tranquilizing drugs, long poles and shotguns. For decades, big-game research had relied on satellites and radio, using telemetry collars placed around the necks of bears. Researchers learned about bear habitats and migratory areas, and with the radios and digital cameras, rangers could not only track an animal, but in daylight were able to see what the bear was foraging. The radios were useful for tracking movements and the location of the camera images. Determining bear's diet required photo images or a physical examination of stomach contents.

The teams set out in their jeeps along a rutted dirt road, and through the woods on the southern tip of the park. Pete was at the wheel and drove to a slope, stopping at a steel drum trap. Alex Hagen drove around them and continued up the hill.

"We've got one," Pete said, pointing to the closed trap door. As they gathered around the trap, the bear banged and shook the steel drum in a violent motion, startling its captors. But it made no other noise. Dave fastened a syringe at the end of a pole and pushed the needle into the bear's rump. The bear whimpered but did nothing else. In less than two minutes, the animal sank to the floor and fell unconscious. Kim opened the trap, while Pete held a shotgun trained on the sleeping bear, and the others helped her pull the beast out of the trap and onto a tarpaulin. The animal had to be over three hundred pounds, a mature boar. It also appeared in good health. They quickly tattooed its inner lip, tagged it, and fastened the collar and camera securely around its neck.

Their final task was to transport the bear to a location closer to the entrance of the park, where Dave suspected the body parts and spice-laden flesh had been spread. The five of them lifted the bear into the vehicle's rear seat.

Hopping into the seat behind Pete, Kim sat fearlessly next to the bear.

"Watch for tongue movements," Dave said, taking the passenger seat in front. "Its eyes are open even though it's out cold."

"You're some lady," Pete quipped. "It takes guts to sit next to a wild bear."

"How long until we get to the release site?" asked Dave.

"About ten minutes," Pete answered. "We should make it."

"Should?" said Kim. "You better not take any longer."

They drove along the trail, rounded a bend in the road, and began to ascend the steep slope leading out of the valley. Suddenly, the jeep began sputtering and soon it ground to a halt.

"Oh, shit!" said Dave.

"What now?" asked Kim.

"Can't get the gears to shift," Pete informed them.

The bear was still sedated, but it had begun moving its head more regularly with every second.

Pete turned off the motor. He waited a few seconds, gave the stick a strong tug, pulled it into PARK and started the engine again. However, the stick jammed and he couldn't get it into DRIVE.

Kim got out of the vehicle and called Alex Hagen in the jeep ahead. In a couple of minutes, she spotted him coming down the slope toward them. The drugged bear farted, coughed and was beginning to move its head drowsily.

"He'll be up before long," Pete said nervously, struggling with the gear shift.

As the bear began to shake and jerk its head, a biologist from Alex's team handed Dave a hypodermic syringe. The dosage subdued the bear's jerkiness and it settled down. Just in case, Dave held onto the door handle, waiting to bolt from the jeep. But the bear's head fell softly down at an angle; the dosage had kicked in at last.

"Oh, my," said Kim. "I don't want to think about what could have happened."

"Let's hurry," said Dave.

Pete was finally able to force the shift into DRIVE, and they once more navigated the trail through the backwoods, followed by the other jeep. As the evening was fading, they stopped near a clearing several miles from the park entrance. The forest was a dark grey, and the alder brush and spruce were blocking the faint light of day's end. They carried the bear out of the jeep and carefully laid it on the ground, lining it up with its feet pointed downward and placing its head on a little pillow of branches and leaves, to prevent it from swallowing its tongue as it revived. The animal began to move its limbs spasmodically, turning and shifting its weight. Its eyes were black and shiny, and they stared out at the people in front of it, as if to silently tell them it knew what they were doing.

Dave checked to see that the camera on the bear's collar was securely fastened and in good working order.

"He should be fully awake soon," he said. "Let's get out of its way."

"I can't wait to see what it's eating," said Alex.

14

Ultimatum

Over the next few days, the task force attached cameras to observe eight bears in their daily foraging. So far, the computer monitor, divided into several viewing areas, had shown nothing out of the ordinary. The sound quality was excellent, and the noises of the animals were as one might expect as they searched the wilds for food.

One afternoon, Alex Hagen turned to the computer and began to stare at a view in the lower corner of the divided screen. Something had caught his attention and he was scrutinizing it nervously, glancing at the others. His eyes widened and he shot a look at Dave, the closest to him, and then quickly at Kim, who was across the room at her desk.

Hagen chuckled and put on a set of earphones attached to the computer, silencing the speakers.

Dave turned to Alex. "What?" And then he saw the image.

"What is it?" Kim asked.

"Oh," said Dave, blushing. "Nothing." The view was of bears mating. Alex handed the earphone set to Dave.

"Let me see," said Kim, as she noticed Dave covering his mouth, trying to suppress a laugh.

"No," said Dave. "You can't, young lady. We're not voyeurs."

"Let me see what you guys are laughing at," Kim insisted.

"Okay," said Alex. "But don't say we didn't warn you."

"Oh, my," Kim laughed when she saw the image. "I'm such an idiot. I should have known. You guys!"

"I expected we'd see some curious sights, but not this!" said Dave, teasing her.

"If bears could talk," said Kim, "they'd tell us we're the problem, not them."

Lovemaking in the wild was not the only view on the computer screen that caught their attention that day. On a top view onscreen, a camera lens held steady on a patch of ground near a log. The bear began moving, the camera swaying as it walked. The sounds first coming from the microphone were of the bear breathing, then growling, before it began clawing and digging. It pulled at debris on the ground, making a hole, or so it seemed. In a few seconds, it had uncovered a dark clump covered with dirt.

"Look!" said Alex. "It's someone's thigh. The bear is eating a person's leg!"

Dave was drawn to the macabre image and saw the dirt-covered object, now revealed by the bear's licking and tearing it apart with its teeth.

"We've got it," said Kim.

Alex wrote down the coordinates displayed on the screen. "I have the location," he said. "We ought to go there now. It's about five miles from the highway truck stop."

Alex took along the laptop with the camera views displayed on the screen. Following the telemetry signal, they drove to where the bear had been dining. By the time they were within a mile of the feeding site, the bear had finished its snack and disappeared into the tuckamore. There were no traces of fresh scat, and Dave thought at first that the location might have been a false one.

Then Dave saw parts of bones in the dirt, and he saw flesh less visible at first glance. He gathered up as much of the material as they could carry in plastic bags. The samples were driven to the airport and flown by charter to St. John's that night.

The next day, the results came over the fax machine in Dave's office. He immediately assembled the team to report the findings.

"A male," said Dave. "It's the flesh of a man about sixty years old who had liver disease."

"Are there any missing persons reported?" Alex asked.

"No," said Dave. "The report states that this body had antibiotics and other medications in it. They have DNA and are checking medical records for local deaths in the last few weeks. That person died of cirrhosis. It was already a corpse when the bear got to it."

Dave thought that Kim would be very surprised by what they had learned. The scat with bone remains was always clean of any intentional contaminant. On the other hand, the scat with the contaminants of pepper and garlic never came with bone fragments. There were two sources of the human fodder: one was showing gross disrespect for human remains and discarding it in a hurry. On the other hand, the remains found far off the beaten path had no bones and contained the deterrent. There were two perpetrators intentionally feeding human remains to bears, but their methods and motives were entirely different.

When Dave called Kim, she was excited. She was in the field, monitoring the camera images on her laptop.

"Check your computer camera views immediately," she demanded. "I can't wait to show you what came up on my screen just a few minutes ago."

Dave gave Kim a summary of the findings he had received from the lab, while Alex looked at the grid of views from the cameras attached to the bears. There, in colour, on the screen were mounds of ground flesh; a bear was grabbing them up and gobbling them down.

"Pay close attention when the bear finishes," said Kim over the phone. "You may see a familiar sight."

A few minutes later, the bear's camera panned the woods. Onscreen was a bear stand with the remains of a scent-bag hanging from a branch.

"Dave, I know this spot," she said. "Remember when I told you about the Crandall guy who was killed by a bear?"

"Yeah."

"The stand has the same construction. It has the same light pine. And it's the same height. I'm driving out there to check it out."

"Tell me what road it's on," said Dave. "I'll meet you there. Don't take any chances, and wait for me."

Kim took things into her own hands and proceeded to the bear stand alone. She confirmed her suspicion right away, calling Dave by cellphone. The stand image saved on the computer was a match. When Dave and Alex's team arrived, following the satellite coordinates, Kim told them she had detected partly covered footprints; the culprit had tried to conceal his tracks as a bear might clear an ambush trail.

Dave turned to the others. "Let's look at a few more sites not far from the highway," he said.

A report had gone to Ottawa and St. John's, and Dave was expecting to receive authorization to step up the public education effort through the media and increase the poster and pamplet campaigns at private businesses and government buildings.

The public were encouraged to report anyone behaving suspiciously in the woods, and who could possibly be dumping garbage of any kind. He would make sure the notices also went out to the forest companies since they logged in remote places where bears commonly roamed.

It was imperative that they find a few younger bears for testing, bears that did not have cameras. Dave would also have to place cameras on many more animals if they were to thoroughly map the area where the flesh was scattered. They would use the park helicopter to avoid trekking through the thick brush. Beating through the heavy growth would waste time, and someone could get killed trying to guess and wait at a site for the person they wanted.

"What if the perpetrator is doing it after dark?" asked Kim. "What can we do then to catch him?"

"We'll install infrared cameras near the sites we already know have been used as drops. That will cover off the possibility of anyone coming back under cover of darkness. These animals like the dark better, and this person knows their habits. He might be an outfitter, a hunter, a woodsman or simply a bear-savvy person. We'll keep checking our screens, tracking and mapping any flesh-eating bears until we can accurately construct their travel patterns."

Over the next few days, the cameras recorded more and more of the feedings at different places, most of them not far from Routes 430 and 431. The cameras showed only a few feedings on dismembered bodies. Nevertheless, the images enabled the sites to be located. Identifying any medications found in a couple of the body parts might find a match to persons who died recently. Dave and his team asked the police and hospitals to search medical records of deaths in the past few weeks. The results threw suspicion on a hospital in Corner Brook and on a couple of funeral homes there. But it also threw suspicion on a mortuary in Deer Lake and another funeral home in Stephenville.

One evening, when Dave returned to his office after supper, he began his regular update of the location map. Kim dropped in after having spent the day putting up posters around the park campsites. Dave called the mortician and arranged to see him at the crematorium within the hour.

Norm Cotten introduced himself to Dave and Kim.

Dave started in right away. "I'd like to ask you a few questions, Mr. Cotten, if I may?"

"Call me Norm. Ask away."

"I was wondering. When a person in Deer Lake dies, how is the body taken care of?"

"Well, the official attending the death would call us. From there it would depend on what the family wanted. For instance, the person could be buried or cremated. The service could be held here or at a church."

"So," Dave said, "you're telling me that the remains are looked after right here?"

"Yes, we have a room for embalming and laying out the deceased for viewing. Cremations are done in a separate room."

"Who does the work?"

"Any one of us could," said Norm, "but usually it's Jack Crandall. My other employee or I would do it if the deceased were a relative or friend of Jack's."

"How long has Jack been working for you?"

"Since last year. Now I have another fellow helping out. The man before him had a heart attack. Young man, too. But digging a grave is hard work. You never know."

"Are there still many plots left at the Deer lake cemetery?" Kim asked.

"Oh, yes," said the mortician. "They will last for years, long after I'm gone."

"Thanks for your help," said Dave. "We may get back to you if we have any further questions. We really appreciate your help."

"Anytime. Have a good one."

As they drove away, Kim mentioned to Dave that something about the funeral home rang a bell. She recalled that Jack Crandall had a connection with Rick Preston.

"I've always liked Jack," she said. "He's a good man who's had a lot of bad luck."

The day was nearly over, so they decided to have supper together at Bob's Big Stop. People were streaming in to pay for gas and purchase smokes and beer, or take a meal in the restaurant.

All plain folk, they looked innocent to Dave and Kim. Many of them they already knew. There was Helen and her husband, Bob, the owner, giggling and telling jokes. Many of the customers were middle-aged, but there were kids there as well. All had a familiar ease with one another, a manner born of long and intimate association in a very small country region on an island where most residents had roots that went back for many generations. They often married their high-school sweethearts, turned up at the legion dances and helped with the little league teams. Nothing about them suggested fiendish or ghoulish minds to Kim. Indeed, when she would try to suggest possible suspects to Dave, she could not come up with anyone she thought could be involved in dismembering and mutilating corpses. The guilty person was not in the restaurant, she was sure.

Asleep in front of his television set, having again fallen asleep during the six o'clock news, Jack was awakened by the ringing of his telephone. It was his boss, Norm, who wanted to see him at the crematorium. Something urgent had come up. He insisted that what he had to discuss with Jack could not wait. He offered to drive to Jack's place, but Jack, fearing Starlight might be lurking about, promptly offered to drive to the funeral home.

When Jack arrived, the front door to Norm's office stood open and the lights were on. Norm was sitting at his desk. He motioned for Jack to sit down.

"I've been wanting to talk to you, Jack," he said. He faced Jack directly, looking into his eyes. "You don't have to worry. You know what I'm about to say."

"Sure, Norm," he said, completely baffled by his boss's statement.

"A biologist and ranger have been by to see me. They were asking questions about this place and about you."

"Why?"

The mortician shook his head. His mouth formed a cynical frown, at once accusatory and irritated.

"Look," he said. "Let me square with you, Jack. I know what you've been doing."

"What are you talking about?"

"Okay," said Norm. "They're on to the bodies you've been taking out of here. I know. Don't look so surprised. You're not the only one who has ever wanted to cut corners around here."

"What are you saying?" Jack was breathing hard, his pulse fierce. But Norm leaned back in his chair, turning a pencil in his hand. Finally, he broke the silence.

"Has everything been all right with you after Dorothy died?" Norm asked.

"Everything is fine."

"That's not what I meant, Jack. Don't play games with me. You have been dismembering corpses, and feeding them as meatballs to the bears. I know you have. Don't think I'm a fool."

Jack began sweating profusely. He saw that further stalling would get Norm seriously riled.

"You don't understand, Norm," he said. "It's not what you think. I had a reason. I was trying to stop the bear attacks. The corpses wouldn't care."

"Nonsense," said Norm. "You couldn't stop the bear attacks alone, you know. I was wondering how long it was going to take for you to tell me. Are you okay for money now?"

"Yeah, I'm fine."

Norm tipped his seat back.

"That's great. Jack, I can help you. You know you could be in serious trouble if this got out. I could lose my licence. You know how people around here would feel about someone mutilating the bodies of their loved ones. They might even take the law into their own hands. You'd get Gros Morne justice, not government justice."

"Why do you want to help me?"

The mortician stared at him, smiling. He told Jack he had worked hard to develop the funeral home and mortuary. He said that he had hired Calvin to help him, because he said he liked him. It had not been easy starting out as a mortician on his own and not joining an established franchise.

"Often there were so many bodies from a family auto accident, a plane crash or boating accident, I had to work night and day, seven days a week," he said. "I was all alone here then and it was exhausting. I worked my ass off to get what I have. I don't want to lose it."

Norm passed him some photographs from an envelope. They were pictures of Jack cutting up mangled body parts to feed into the grinder. There was Jack, making his special bear recipe and storing it in pails for carrying.

"I have been watching you for some time," said Norm, "but don't worry. I'm not going to say anything. I want you to play ball with me, Jack. I want you to do as I say."

"What do you want, Norm?"

"Nothing," said the mortician. "Only, I may need you to continue disposing of bodies in the woods every now and then, say, as a favour to me. It costs too much to burn them. And the ones from out of the province are a nuisance. I want to cut costs."

"But you're asking for trouble," said Jack. "You said they're asking questions here."

"Let me handle them," said Norm. "I'm going to decide when to get rid of a few cremation jobs. I'll save a bundle in energy bills. The government or insurance companies will pay the cremation invoices, as long as I provide the certificate. You'll be helping me, as I am helping you stay out of trouble."

Jack nodded slowly.

"See you tomorrow," said Norm.

"Good night," said Jack.

When he got to work the next day, there was a truckload of coffins to be stored in a garage out back. Next, there were a couple of bodies waiting for disposal.

Norm got down to business. He pointed to dismembered bodies scheduled for cremation.

"Take the parts to the woods tonight," he said. "Nobody is going to claim their ashes."

"Sure," said Jack. "But why not cremate them?"

"Because I don't want to make money the old-fashioned way. Like I told you yesterday, Jack, I want to cut down on my energy expenses."

Jack was dumbstruck. Norm was making a bundle by skipping cremations and getting paid for them. Of the two of them, Norm was worse for having profited from Jack's ghoulish activities. Now he realized why Norm had made him take time off some weeks ago; it was so his boss could install hidden cameras in the crematorium to observe Jack handling the bodies. And now he was being blackmailed.

What could he expect to get in return for carrying out Norm's wishes? And how could it be done? The rangers were on to the corpses and the spiked meat, and it was only a matter of time before the trail led them to the funeral home. He remembered how he had witnessed greed blinding very intelligent men in the woods—professionals like doctors and lawyers on his outfitting trips. He recalled the many smart men he had known making very stupid mistakes, some losing their lives as a result. He resolved not to take any more risks while the investigation was going on.

If they came to him, he could blame Mark for any dismemberment and mutilation of body parts identified from the funeral home. Yes, Mark could have done it, he thought, unless they found parts recently. He stopped in sudden fear. Not only would the funeral home be watched, the forests would be full of rangers and police watching and tailing anyone working at funeral homes in the area.

Fear flooded his mind, penetrating his entire body as well, the fear of the guilty, the fear of being discovered, the fear of further public humiliation. He began to panic at the thought of being charged. Well, if he went down, he would take that greedy bastard funeral director with him.

Jack's anger at Norm did not displace his fear. He had to get out of this, somehow. Quitting his job would not end his problem with Norm. If he quit, then he could expect the police to visit him right after Norm gave them the photographs. He was in a mess. A real dilemma. There had to be a way out. He would have to talk to Norm, and persuade him that this was too dangerous. After all, Jack, as a woodsman, knew how small an obstacle the forest could be to determined hunters. He knew also how difficult—if not impossible—it would be to evade them. It would be dangerous to even go back into the woods with any human flesh—far too dangerous to them both.

He got into his protective clothing and began cremating the body that Norm had told him to cut up and dump in the woods. He felt satisfied and emboldened for having defied his boss. When he finished, he labelled the ashes and stored them away. He began cleaning the crematorium tables and sinks and swept and mopped the flooor.

Norm would be in later that day, he thought, and he would see what Jack had done. Jack expected Norm to be displeased, but he would plead with him to put an end to this crazy scheme. Norm would surely see that this was the right thing to do. Even if he was a thief as well as a ghoul, the mortician was not stupid.

15

Starlight

At suppertime that day, Jack drove to Bob's Big Stop in Deer Lake. Since his wife's death, he had taken to eating at the café a few times a week. There he would greet the old-timers who gathered for a coffee and yarn. Most of the time, he took his food alone, sitting at a table in a corner of the restaurant, reading his newspaper.

"Good day, Jack," said Helen. She placed a hand on his shoulder. "What are you up to today?"

"Nothing much, Helen. I have my good days and my bad, like everyone else."

"You hear the news?"

"What news?" he said, unfolding the newspaper.

"It's not in there," she laughed. "They're always late with the news around here. I meant the news about the garlic and pepper someone's been feeding the bears. Maybe that's why there haven't been any attacks reported lately, huh?"

"No," Jack replied. "I hadn't heard. Is that what they're saying?"

"Oh, yes. One of the girls in the mayor's office came down this afternoon and gave us the scoop. Said she wasn't supposed to be quoted, as if we would keep it a secret here. You know, what's she blabbing it here for if she wanted to keep it quiet? But now the whole town knows. It'll be in *The Western Gazette* tomorrow, I bet you."

"Interesting," said Jack.

"How about a cup of coffee?"

"Sure."

As he ate his supper, he began reading *The Western Gazette*'s editorial page. Again there was a searing denunciation of the Parks Department for not getting to the bottom of the bear attacks. OFF THE HOOK! the headline read.

> "We continue to make idle threats and get no action. If the Parks Department doesn't get its act together in finding out why the bears have attacked so many people here, there will be no more tourism season for a long time. Newfoundlanders deserve better treatment."

Below the editorial was the invitation, "Tell Us What You Think." Jack considered writing a letter telling the editor that the government was not the solution to the problem, but he knew it would be of no use. It might even draw more attention to him.

When he returned to his house, he found Starlight roaming about the lawn grubbing for insects. Soon the bear would start more intensive feeding, in preparation for hibernation. Jack wondered whether he should let him feed in the garden, and prepare the den in the shed so Starlight would not be disturbed. But the bear, he thought, would soon find another den when it became independent that year and no longer wanted Jack's companionship. While he pondered this question, he heard the telephone ring in the house. It was Norm. He said he had called earlier and left a few messages.

"I'd like to see you."

"I'm about to turn in," said Jack. "Been a long day for me."

"It won't take long," said Norm.

"Okay," said Jack. "You can come now."

Norm had never been to Jack's cottage. In the evening the property had a vacant, funereal austerity, and outside, the garden was overrun with weeds. Starlight was in the shed napping when Norm arrived. Jack greeted his boss, and the two men sat on the verandah watching the evening light fade into darkness.

"You drove out of your way," said Jack. "This must be important."

"Well, now," said Norm, "I'm glad you noticed that time is important to me. That's a nice shed. Build it yourself?"

"Yes," said Jack, "I built it when we moved here last year. But you didn't come all the way out here to compliment me about my handiwork. What's on your mind, Norm?"

"I thought we had an agreement."

"I think we'd be nuts to drop any bodies in the woods right now, with all that's going on," said Jack. "Haven't you read the papers? The place is crawling with constabulary and rangers. They have all kinds of ways of catching poachers. They won't have much of a problem finding us. It's too big a risk right now. Maybe later in the fall before the bears hibernate, when there's not so many people around the park."

"What about up north?" asked Norm. "Nobody goes up there, not even in the fall."

"You know, Norm, I think I'm the wrong man for this kind of business. I don't think it's going to work for me. If you want to get rid of cremations that way, get somebody else."

Norm sat in silent meditation for a few moments. Finally, he opened his eyes, turned to Jack, and smiled.

"Yes," he said. "You're probably right, Jack. But I'd hate to get you into trouble."

"You're trying to blackmail me. You could have trouble, too."

"I would be doing my duty as a law-abiding person," said Norm. "No one would believe you, in any event."

"Hey, Norm, I'm a free man."

"That you are," said Norm. "Think about it. Freedom."

He rose from the chair, preparing to leave.

"Later," Jack said. "Do it later in the fall."

"I know it's safe up north," Norm said. "Those bears eat meat all the time."

"Think about it," said Jack. "But count me out."

"What gratitude! We'll see," Norm said as he walked toward the shed.

Jack followed as his boss sized up the property.

"It's a nice spot," Norm muttered. "It needs sprucing up, but it'd make a nice summer place for me."

"I'm not interested in selling it."

Norm stepped inside the shed and turned on a light. "Whew! It stinks in here. What do you use it for?"

"Workshop," said Jack.

"I guess you won't have to come to work tomorrow. I'm going to get this place at an auction after I deliver you to the police."

"Get out of here!" Jack screamed, pushing Norm to the door. "Get the hell out of here and take that job and shove it up your ass!"

Norm began walking to his car in the evening light, when suddenly he was grabbed from behind. Starlight picked him up by the back of his jacket and shook him.

"Help!" Norm screamed as Starlight flung him to the ground. "Help me!"

"No!" Jack shouted.

He was giving the signal for Starlight to back off, but the bear held Norm down and began to lick his face and clothes.

"Call it off, Jack," Norm begged.

"Where are the videos and photographs that you were going to use against me?"

"I'll give them all to you. They're in a safe at the office."

"What's the combination to your safe?"

"It's in the drawer in my desk. It's taped in back of the drawer on the top left."

"Are there any copies?" asked Jack.

"No. I didn't want any of that stuff lying around anywhere."

"You must have another safe deposit box in the office," said Jack.

"Yes. Why?"

"Give me the key."

"For what?"

"I said give me the key."

"It's in the glove compartment with my car keys."

Jack searched the compartment.

"Thank you, Norm. Tomorrow we'll get rid of the photos."

"You'll see," gasped Norm, "I'm not lying. Now get this bear off of me."

When Norm was clear of Starlight, he walked to his black Mercedes, got inside and searched the glove compartment. Jack and Starlight were watching him from the shed. Norm got out of the car and came over to them again.

"You took my car keys."

"Yes," said Jack.

"Well, I can't drive without them."

"I know," said Jack.

"Give me my damned car keys."

"It's too late for you to drive. Why don't you sleep here, and tomorrow we'll take care of the photographs."

"I don't think so," said Norm, pulling out a shiny silver revolver. "Now, Jack, give me my car keys."

"Get out of here, get!" said Jack, as Starlight once again jumped on the undertaker. Norm fired his pistol, striking Starlight. The bear, infuriated by the shot, took Norm's face in his mouth and ripped away a large piece of flesh and bone.

"No," Jack pleaded weakly.

The bear relented, backing off and limping. Norm was lying on the ground, moaning, still conscious. When Jack approached Starlight, the bear growled at him.

"Let me see, Starlight! Move!"

But the bear only flattened his ears back. Starlight's mouth went forward, the hair on his back bristling. Jack decided not to push his luck. A wounded animal, even a domesticated dog, could be dangerous to its lifelong owner. The bear turned and entered the shed and lay down on his bed of saplings and brush.

Jack watched from a few feet away. It looked as though Norm's shot had entered his shoulder and exited without breaking any bones. It didn't seem a serious wound, but the bear had lost blood. As Jack approached cautiously, the bear growled. He waited, then reached out and touched Starlight. He moved, but did not look at Jack. The hair below the wound was caked with half-dried blood.

Starlight continued to snarl whenever Jack touched his wound. After a few minutes, the bear got up and immediately lay down on the ground in the shed. He rose again, sat on his haunches, and once again slumped to the ground. Jack gave him a pan of water, but Starlight flipped it across the shed with his snout. Jack handed him an old, chewed-up blanket, but the bear sniffed indifferently at it. The bear's mouth was half-opened, crusted with blood from licking his wound and Norm's mangled face. Jack knew that bears had a tremendous immune system and wonderful powers of recovery. Starlight would just need some time to recover from the gunshot.

As the minutes passed, the bear began to make sounds. Between panting and groaning, he turned over to face Jack. At length, Starlight closed his eyes and fell asleep. Jack sat there rubbing the fur on the bear's soft woolly head, and soon Starlight was resting easily.

Outside the shed, Norm lay on the ground, his face and chest covered in blood, but he was still breathing. Jack's pulse raced as he wondered what to do next. He went into the house and rummaged through a large trunk. "Ah," he said to himself, grabbing a bag in a closet and opening it. He pulled out a couple of bear paws that a taxidermist had made for him a few years back.

"These will do."

He went back inside the shed and checked on Starlight, who was still asleep and breathing regularly. He stuffed a few clumps of scat and a woollen blanket with clots of his fur stuck to it into a plastic bag and placed it in Norm's car trunk. He spread out a blanket on the back seat of Norm's car, laid the funeral director across the seat, and drove to the funeral home.

Behind the funeral parlour, Jack made impressions of the bear paws on the ground and collected some blood from Norm's arm with a hypodermic. He sprayed the blood around the bear footprints and shook fur from Starlight's blanket onto the ground. He took Norm's semi-conscious body and scuffed it around the prints, before returning to the car and placing him in the passenger's seat.

There was one more essential task.

Jack went into the funeral home, pulled out the drawer to Norm's desk and wrote down the code to Norm's safe. He went to the safe in the corner and manipulated the combination lock until the door clicked inside and popped. On a shelf, he found the envelope containing the photographs and several videotapes. In the corner of the office, covered with a rust-stained cloth, was what seemed to be a large metal cabinet. When he approached it, he heard the faint hum of a motor. He removed the cloth to find a freezer underneath. He had not paid much attention to Norm's office when he was there earlier, and had taken no notice of his boss's choice of furniture. When he opened the freezer, his mouth dropped. Inside, carefully organized on shelves were plastic containers marked to identify the contents: EYES, KIDNEYS, TEETH, LIVERS.

"My God!" he breathed. "So Norm was keeping parts of corpses he didn't cremate. Probably trying to sell them on the black market."

This meant that Norm had something to hide from the police as well. Jack put the bag and contents back in the freezer. Then he took the photographs and videotapes outside and got in Norm's Mercedes.

He raced Norm's car to the hospital in Corner Brook, with Norm sitting half-conscious beside him covered in clotted blood.

Jack explained to the emergency doctor in attendance that he had found Norm at the rear of the funeral home in Deer Lake, bleeding, seemingly from a bear attack. He left Norm there and went to the police station in Deer Lake to make out a bear-attack report. That done, he drove home. He checked in on Starlight and then burned the photographs and videotapes in an oil drum.

The next day he went to the hospital to check on Norm. The nurse in attendance on the floor told Jack that Norm was heavily sedated and receiving blood transfusions and antibiotics around the clock. Every now and then, he would wake up and have seizures of delirium. The nurse added that Norm had asked to have the bandages removed so he could see the damage to his face.

"He is badly disfigured," she said. "Lost his nose, an eye and an ear. Most of his lower jaw is also gone. Frankly, Mr. Crandall, I don't know if he's going to make it."

It was better that Norm died this way, he thought.

When he returned in the evening to check on Norm, he learned the grim news that he had died, but perversely, a heavy weight lifted from Jack's shoulders.

"Norm insisted that we have his life-support system removed," the doctor said. "He was able to see his face, and after looking at himself, he said that he was so disfigured that he didn't want to live with his injuries. The moment he was alone, he pulled out his transfusion and medication drips. He died before the nurse checked in on him. And he died before we could do anything."

At the shed, Starlight greeted Jack with a woof as he entered the makeshift den. When Jack reached out to pat his head, the bear licked his hand with gratitude and affection. Soon Starlight lifted himself stiffly on his haunches, pawing the air like a hungry dog. Jack fetched a moose roast from his refrigerator and fed it to Starlight, then refreshed the bear's water. Starlight seemed no worse for his ordeal. He was healing rapidly, yet still showed his dominant, assertive character, growling at Jack when he wanted to be left alone.

In a week, Starlight was back to normal and foraging in the woods; he was eating roots and berries, ants and grass, and the remains of both wild and garden vegetables.

Each morning, Jack stopped by Bob's Big Stop for doughnuts and coffee. He had nothing to do, now that another funeral home in Corner Brook was buying Norm's business. The mortuary was presently closed for renovations, and the new owner was planning to reopen for business in a month.

Jack was about to read his morning paper, when he glanced up from his table to see Helen in front of him.

"Oh, Jack!" she said. "Will it never end?"

She poured him some coffee.

"What?"

"I've lived here all my life, but I never would have believed such things could happen around here."

"What are you talking about?"

"You know. The news about Norm and the funeral home. It's even in the paper this morning." And she unfolded the front page of the paper and laid it on the table.

Jack's face flushed as he read.

FUNERAL HOME SEIZED BY POLICE AND PARK DEPARTMENT IN CRIMINAL INVESTIGATION

DEER LAKE——Nearly four months after authorities began searching for the cause of numerous bear attacks in the area, the mystery appears to have been solved. Police and rangers raided a Deer Lake crematorium, formerly owned by the late Norm Cotten, and have hauled away bodies and body parts. The business site has become a crime scene. The new owners deny any prior knowledge of unprofessional or criminal conduct.

The Royal Canadian Mounted Police's Special Investigation Unit from St. John's and park rangers aided by park biologists report that the home has been under suspicion of mutilating human remains. Now they have added embezzlement and falsifying death certificates, authorities said.

The allegations in police reports state that Mr. Cotten may have been taking bodies entrusted to him for purposes of cremation or burial and dismembering them before scattering them in and around Gros Morne National Park to feed to bears. "This made the bears accustomed to human flesh in their diet, causing them to attack people as prey," Ranger Kim Hollings said.

Anyone involved in this activity could face up to ten years in prison.

The investigation into the bear attacks has been time-consuming, involving the analysis of many samples and documents, park officials said.

"After the police seized and secured the funeral home," Hollings said, "they ensured that every single one of those bodies had the proper identification and proper paperwork with it."

Along with the crematory, the funeral home provided burial services for indigent persons who could not afford such services.

Part of the mortuary service was to provide what are called "willed bodies" for medical and educational research.

If the family of a deceased person wished to be part of that program, which started about a year ago, they had to sign a form that released the body to Mr. Cotten. If, after a blood test, it was determined that the body had no communicable diseases, it was turned over to a medical researcher who then decided how it would be used in research.

According to authorities, some of the bodies that had been referred to Cotten's business, either by private parties or the state, were intended to be either cremated or buried, but were not.

Park biologist Dave Bishop said that the twenty-one bodies seized as evidence in the case would be released to other mortuaries.

Bishop said authorities have identified ten of the bodies by name, and eleven others are yet to be identified through a check of Cotten's business records. Those bodies and body parts are currently specified only by number while investigators continue to try and determine who they were.

"The case is ongoing," Hollings said.

"Usually," Hollings added, "[authorities] will arrest someone immediately after we suspect probable cause because they are a flight risk or a danger to the community. But the unusual circumstances of the investigation into a novel animal problem delayed us considerably in identifying the funeral home as the location of the problem."

Hollings added that the rangers and police decided to act on their investigation following the death of Mr. Cotten from a bear attack a few days ago. They determined there was sufficient evidence to obtain search warrants and inspect the funeral home.

16

Out of Time

"The whole island is upset," said Helen, when she returned to take Jack's order.

Jack just nodded. He felt compelled to deny any association with the allegations in the paper.

"I didn't see any bodies at Cotten's that weren't supposed to be there," Jack said to Helen. "It was really no different than any other funeral home. Nothing you heard said anything about bodies found outside the home, huh?"

"I heard something," she said. "I heard a cleaner was in Norm's house and found a body bag stuffed under his bed."

"We're shocked something like that could happen here," said Arthur, a local electrician sitting in the next booth, who overheard the conversation. "It's another black eye for funeral services. Danny Moore reported his mother Bertha Ferolle missing from her casket when they dug it up."

Helen left the table and Jack sat alone, eating a breakfast of pancakes and ham. In the background, he overheard people's disbelief and anger.

"You would never think something like this could happen here; it's a little bitty town," said Helen, back to refill Jack's cup.

Her husband Bob joined in. "Relatives of some of those whose bodies have already been identified plan to hold meetings at a church near the crematorium and in Stephenville, to compare horror stories and comfort each other."

"I'd just like to get a hold of that guy," said Arthur. "You know, I've been in and out of the crematorium on various jobs, and I've never noticed any signs of bodies not being handled properly."

He gave Jack a thumbs-up, but Jack felt the gesture was insincere.

Arthur continued talking. "I have to wonder about poor Trevor Barney. He died in June, and his body was supposed to have been cremated. Dave Woodman told me his mother died in May, and if he finds out her body was fed to the bears, he'll burn the mortuary down and kill everyone responsible. The urn supposed to be filled her ashes sits on a mantle, adorned with flowers. I heard two bodies were found stacked in a garage on the funeral home property.

"Somebody'd better be going to jail. There are more people involved, I bet. Norm wasn't in this all by himself. I bet some of the other funeral home directors around here were doing this, too."

Jack could not endure listening to any more of this gossip, as much of the anger seemed directed at him. How could he respond? What could he say? All he wanted to do was leave. He hurriedly paid for his meal, waved to Helen and the others, and left the café.

He drove by the mortuary and saw a police car parked outside. He could imagine the headlines the next day: FUNERAL HOME WORKER CHARGED IN MUTILATIONS AND FEEDING HUMAN BODY PARTS TO BEARS. At that moment, he wished he were in another country. He was so agitated, he was trembling.

When he arrived home, Starlight was gone, so Jack took the opportunity to clean and sand the barn's claw-marked door. By noon, he had smoothed the wood, filled in where the bear had dug for roots, and replaced Starlight's broken saplings. He had also cleaned traces of the bear's paths in the garden, as well as most of the prints and scat in the field around his house. He scraped off any of Starlight's molts he could find on the nearby tree trunks.

Now that Dorothy and Calvin were gone, his career as an outfitter finished and his job at the mortuary gone as well, it would not be so difficult for Jack to leave. He might have to answer some questions from the rangers and police, and he wondered whether he would be considered an accessory to whatever offences had been laid against Norm. His boss was now safely beyond the reach of the law, thanks to Starlight. He shrugged. He probably would be charged. Even if he wasn't, he felt certain he would be suspected, whispered about and ostracized, no matter what else developed regarding the funeral home. No question about it; he would be unwelcome in Deer Lake and Corner Brook for a long time.

But where could he go?

Before him, in the distance, lay the wilderness of the north. There meandered beryl-blue fjords and lakes deep between the snow-crested mountains, dotted with tall green conifers that rose into the sky. There were lush valleys, an abundance of fish and wildlife, and the dark green range of Gros Morne Tablelands. The forest hid everything beneath its cover. A man could get lost there, live and die there, and no one would ever find him. He could find plentiful game animals, rabbits, birds and squirrels, and in a valley, with a little seed, he could grow crops and vegetables. It would take only two days by hiking to get to a pleasant valley and remove oneself from humanity. Jack recalled one time finding pictographs and paintings from ancient Canadian Indians showing bears and humans in one of the caves along the mountains, still hidden from the world.

He thought of what he would need and what he would have to leave behind for such a trip. He would see bears, caribou and many moose, so he would be sure to bring along Norm's pistol, his own shotgun and plenty of ammo. The route would be simple, following a fjord through the southern tip of the park to a river and then to a wildly dashing stream, zigzagging and crossing land to another body of water in the wild vastness east and north. The mountains would be impenetrable to most hikers, so encountering another person on the trek would not be likely. And what about Starlight?

Transplanting a strange bear into another bear's territory was asking for trouble, primarily for the transplanted bear. Most woodsmen knew this bit of lore. On the other hand, Starlight would have Jack as a companion. He could help him acquire territory by displacing other resident bears. They could establish a place where they could live together. He could travel fifty miles using good-sized backpacks with some water, food supplies, tools and a shotgun. He'd carry one, Starlight the other two strapped over his back.

It was September; Jack could feel the slide to autumn in his bones already. The western sky would be full of stars hanging like bright blue Christmas tree lights on a dark canopy; he would shiver in the cool headwinds off the rivers beneath them. The very thought of the cold was daunting. Jack took a deep breath and exhaled. He would leave sometime that night, or as soon as Starlight awakened on his tree branch and returned to the shed. He began packing tools into his truck. He put a few kitchen utensils aboard, and packed away several months worth of supplies and staples: flour, baking powder, rice, vegetable seeds. He carried the backpacks of food into the back of his truck. In the shed he found the guns and ammo he had kept hidden after his conviction. He also selected other tools to take with him: axes, saws, a portable wood stove, nails and a hammer. When he was done, he sat in the house and waited for Starlight.

Later that evening, he thought he heard sounds outside. Perhaps it was just the patter of rain beginning to fall. He listened. No, it was not rain, he decided, but the beginning of autumn breezes rustling dried maple leaves. The late summer had gradually slid into fall.

Jack heard the rumble of a vehicle pulling into his drive. He looked up and saw Dave Bishop and Kim Hollings climb out of a park jeep.

"Good evening, Jack," the female ranger said as he came outside. "I see you're packing your truck. Planning a trip?"

"Maybe," said Jack. "Thought I might try St. John's for work. What can I do for you?"

Kim peered into Jack's truck. Dave looked over at piles of garbage bags Jack had filled from cleaning the barn and around his house.

"Going for long?" asked Dave.

"Maybe."

"If you don't mind, Jack," said Kim, "I'd like to look around here. It's no reflection on you, but this is an area we have not looked at earlier."

"Sure, help yourself. You don't have a warrant, I guess. This is not an investigation, right?"

"That's right," said Dave.

The scientist walked over to the edge of the field and examined the bark on the trees.

"Kim," he said, "Would you come here for a minute?"

Dave and Kim talked quietly, out of earshot. Jack wanted to approach them, but something in him told him not to do so; the conversation was clearly meant not to include him. They finished their conversation and walked over to him.

"Seemed like some pretty serious talk," said Jack.

"Yes," said Kim. "Dave was asking me about the bear writing on the bark of the trees. It looks fresh to me. Have you seen any bears around here recently?"

"You're kidding, right? I'd have someone make me a nice rug if I did."

"Do you mind if I show Dave your shed?"

"Not at all," Jack said with a broad grin. "Would you not look there if I objected?"

"Thanks, Jack," she said. "Come with us, please."

Inside the shed, they inspected the slight depression in the ground where Starlight slept, and they observed the fresh paint on the walls that covered his claw marks.

"How many bodies did you do a week for Norm Cotten?" she asked.

"Probably three or four. We would service the whole side of the island. But I didn't know anything about what Norm was doing."

"We know," said Dave. "Norm's records and the human organs we found in his fridge incriminated him. He had been mutilating corpses for a long time and getting away with not cremating them. He wouldn't have wanted you to cremate people if he was profiting from it."

"It must have bothered you," said Kim, "cremating people you knew."

"Not really," Jack said. "If I knew the person, or if it was a close friend or family, yeah, it would bother me. Then Norm would do …" He stopped in mid-sentence. "Norm was probably cheating me too. He took care of Dorothy and Calvin for me, so I thought. But he may have fed them to the bears. I never would have guessed before you just suggested it. That scoundrel! He was nothing but a fiend. No good sonofabitch."

"None of us knew him," Kim said, "though everybody thought they did. I often wonder whether any of us actually knows who anyone is inside."

"That's true," said Dave. "But you know, while Norm was feeding bodies to the bears, someone else was feeding garlic-and-pepper packs in ground human meat to them as well. It was to stop the bears from eating human flesh, to stop Norm from creating dangerous predators in the park, we suspect. Whoever it was ought to be treated as a hero."

"Yes," said Kim. "We haven't heard of any more bear attacks since we started finding the deterrent packs in bear stomachs and scat."

"You sure keep it clean in here, Jack," Dave observed.

"So tourists will come back. Thank goodness! Whoever was putting down the garlic-and-pepper snacks for the bears should be congratulated."

"It's against the law, though," Kim reminded him.

"What do you keep in this pail?" asked Dave.

"All kinds of stuff. Deep fryer grease, molasses, doughnuts, pig's intestines, blood."

"Blood?" asked Dave. "Where would you get the blood?"

"At the butcher shop. When they slaughter the pigs or beef cattle, I'd get the owner to save it for me. The smell is hard to remove. So is the colour."

"What do you use blood and meat scrapings for?" asked Kim.

"For a worm bed I have for fishing," said Jack.

"You know," Kim said, "I would never have thought to use pepper and garlic in rubber or plastic and put it in ground meat to feed to bears. I would have never thought of that."

"Hey," Jack said, "it's hard to believe it would work."

Kim and Dave walked around the shed and returned to the lawn and the garden.

"Sorry to bother you, Jack," said Dave when they came back around. "We have to run."

An hour later, Starlight arrived at the verandah door. Jack was inside labelling boxes, having a beer and listening to the news. When he heard the bear woofing, he went out to it immediately.

"Come along, you," he said, heading to the shed with Starlight behind him. "This is your last time sleeping here. We leave at dawn."

Jack mixed a little honey in the bear's moose meat. He figured it would make Starlight sleepy. But when the bear finished eating, he appeared at the verandah door again. It seemed to Jack that he wanted company and sensed that they were leaving their home for good.

Back in the shed, Jack fed the bear another moose joint, figuring now that a gorged bear was a sleepy bear. But Starlight walked out of the shed to the house once more, as though to tell Jack that he was not going to rest until he had gotten some attention from him. Finally, on that cool evening, Starlight ate his third moose joint, then lay down in the shed to sleep. He turned in his earthen bed, filling the small indentation with his furry back. He snoozed soundly for two hours as Jack packed and labelled the rest of the boxes for their trip. In a cooler, he stored smoked salmon and trout. He rushed to fill the skiff mounted on a trailer hitched to his truck. In addition to his firearms, he included a bear bow, arrows and Aldrich snares, along with candles. He tossed his skis and snowshoes in the skiff, along with a heavy canvas tent.

By eleven o'clock, most of what he would need was tucked away in the vehicle. Jack sat in the chaise lounge on the verandah, thinking he would rouse Starlight soon. He dozed a little, but soon he came to. He didn't know what had awakened him. He stood, rubbed the sleep out of his eyes, and walked outside with flashlight in hand, its light turned off.

Jack heard movement and thought it was only Starlight stirring in the shed. He was about to turn around, when he saw a brilliant light illuminating dark silhouettes of trees near the road. It was a motor vehicle. Someone was either paying him a visit or they were lost. He waited in the yard as the beams of the headlamps got closer. Suddenly, the lights went black and the sound of the engine stopped. Jack estimated the vehicle to be no more than a couple of hundred yards away as he stood there waiting. The lights came on again and the engine started up. Maybe the driver had gotten out to take a leak or check a map.

The twin beams drew closer, revealing the trees and the dirt road as the vehicle approached. Then it turned into Jack's driveway. The headlamps went out as it stopped only a few feet in front of him. It was the same park jeep that had visited him earlier. Out of the car stepped Dave Bishop, holding two cups of coffee. He was alone.

"Hello, Jack," he said, handing him a cup of coffee. "I figured you'd be up late packing. It's cream with no sugar. I hope that's okay."

"Sure," said Jack. "Thanks."

"I forgot to ask you a couple of more questions. I need to finish my report tonight. Last-minute business."

"Well," Jack said uneasily, "you can see I'm busy."

"It'll only take a few minutes," Dave said. "I didn't call you because I wanted to ask you in person."

"What's that?"

"You know," said Dave. "I never would have thought of the garlic-and-pepper deterrent. I'm aware of HALT, the stuff everyone splatters on things. But pepper and garlic wrapped in saran wrap? Never."

"Listen, Dave," Jack said. "I'm really busy. If you want, I'll answer your questions when I get back from my trip this fall."

"Jack," Dave said, shaking his head, "this is a mess."

"What do you mean?"

"The pail used for blood, the garlic. Funny thing, Jack. I guess you knew enough about all of this to know it worked. Why didn't you tell us about feeding the bears the garlic-and-pepper meat packs when we came here earlier?"

17

Twilight, Starlight

"Get off my property." Jack turned and walked to the verandah door. Dave followed him. The two men stood in the silver moonlight. Surrounding the clearing was a dense forest which night painted solidly black below the shiny treetops.

Jack turned his flashlight on Dave and the cup of coffee in his hand. Dave almost seemed resentful that his suspect was Jack. In his voice and manner, there had been something resembling regret.

The man's accusations, of course, had struck Jack as impudent and brazen. They were, Jack knew, based on circumstantial evidence. For a park biologist to come to his house without a warrant or arrest powers was downright illegal, an abuse of government authority. What next? The government walking into your bedroom, and bureaucrats taxing you for inspecting your house?

Jack reasoned that with Norm's death there was nothing to tie him to any of the corpse dismemberments and the feeding of human remains to the bears. The Crown would have a difficult time making a case against him. First, there would have to be formal charges, a warrant for his arrest, an arraignment; he knew the game well by this time. A trial would be a mess, however. It would also mean no trip to the north in the fast approaching dawn. No, he thought, there could be no trial. He turned off his flashlight.

"I'm asking you nicely, Dave. Get off my property right now."

"No, Jack. Besides Norm and Mark, you were the only one free all these past months, the only other person who could have disposed of the bodies."

"Get out of here," said Jack, more softly. "I'm about to call it a night."

"I thought you were the fall guy," said Dave. "But when I saw the grinder in the funeral home and smelled the garlic, I knew what was going on."

He walked to the shed, and in the darkness, Jack heard him open the door. It was as though the evidence were waiting for Dave to bring before an invisible jury, to convince them of Jack's guilt.

"Here's all the proof I need," Dave said.

"Leave!" Jack shouted, approaching the shed. "Close that door!"

He was just a few feet away from Dave when they both heard the movement of something heavy inside. The last thing Dave recalled was light exploding inside his head as the bear knocked him unconscious.

"No!" Jack shouted at Starlight.

The bear was standing on all fours, towering over a prone and helpless Dave. It had begun licking him, but Jack's command worked, and Starlight broke into a sprint and dashed behind the shed and into the deep woods, the sounds of his heavy feet breaking dry limbs fading into the darkness.

A spotlight blazed on the shed from the road as the emergency lights from a second jeep shone into the yard. Kim leaped from the jeep and hit the ground running, holding her .44 pistol on Jack.

"Stand away, Jack," Kim said, her gun trained on him as she spoke through a mike attached to her shoulder.

A powerful beam of light came over the trees from the horizon, followed by the muffled beat of chopper blades. Within minutes, the aircraft landed on Jack's lawn. Two policemen jumped out, one rushing over to help Dave to his feet; the other circled the shed, his shotgun braced against his shoulder, sweeping the surrounding trees.

"This is Captain Hann and Sergeant Cook," Kim said to Jack. "They have something for you."

"We're with the RCMP," Captain Hann said. "We have a warrant for your arrest, Jack Crandall. You are charged with mutilating and dismembering human corpses. You have the right to remain silent. Anything you do say can and will be used against you in a court of law. You have the right to an attorney. If you cannot afford one, one will be appointed to you. Please accompany Ranger Hollings and myself to the Deer Lake detachment."

The captain handcuffed Jack and escorted him to Kim's jeep; Dave, feeling wobbly and unable to drive, climbed into the vehicle also. Sergeant Cook departed in the chopper.

Jack's house was once again shrouded in darkness. Not a sound coming from the black forest that surrounded the cleared land.

After Dave filled out his report at the detachment office, he found Jack in the booking station with Kim, Captain Hann, and Sergeant Cook. The sergeant was taking Jack's personal information and completing a form.

"Excuse me, Kim," said Dave, "I'd like a word with Jack."

"Sure," she said.

"I just want to say, Jack," he said, "I'm sorry how things turned out for you. But thanks for saving my life."

"Sure."

"That will be noted at trial, I assure you. One other thing, Jack," Dave said. "The flower in the scat ... where did it come from? And why did you put it in?"

Jack described how Dorothy had found the plant in the Tablelands, and the time it blew into King's food dish. "I figured it might affect the bears faster," he explained.

Sergeant Cook advised Jack that he would be held overnight for an appearance before a magistrate in the morning, who would decide whether or not he'd be released. The policeman led him to his cell.

Outside, Kim and Dave walked to her jeep. He had left his vehicle at Jack's and planned to retrieve it in the morning.

"Thanks, Kim. You were right."

"When you told me about the garlic odour in the funeral home grinder, I knew it was him," she said.

They both agreed on one thing: Norm had not been feeding the bears the spiked flesh. The cameras had shown freshly distributed flesh balls filled with garlic; these locations were difficult to access, and too challenging for someone with Norm's physique. Additionally, he simply didn't have the time.

"As an outfitter, Jack knew this deterrent worked with moose and caribou meat for years. It was easy for him to come up with the anti-bear tactic," said Dave.

As the two headed for Kim's vehicle, he replayed how it was done. The plastic-wrapped deterrent was buried in a casing of human-tainted meat. The bears would eat it, unaware of the pepper-and-garlic-laced core, and later the animal would develop a severe stomach ache which they would associate with the taste of the human-flavoured hamburger.

"Yes," said Kim. "It worked. We haven't had a call in weeks reporting that a bear has eaten someone."

"Jack was your first choice," Dave asked her. "Wouldn't you say?"

"Well, yes."

"So you thought he was guilty of planting the flesh mounds?"

"Yeah, I guess I did," she said.

The two of them fell silent. Dave, resting his head against the headrest, closed his eyes.

"Too bad," he said after a long silence.

"You mean for Jack," said Kim.

"And for the families."

"We can't help their loved ones.".

"Jack is the one in trouble," said Dave.

"He did save your life. I would never have made it to help you before that bear broke your neck, Dave."

"It may help his case."

"It may," she said.

"Have you any idea what he's facing if convicted?" Dave asked.

"They will fine him seven thousand dollars," Kim said. "If the judge factors in his previous conviction, he could get five years."

"Jail would kill him," said Dave. "He wouldn't survive a month cooped up in a cell."

"Don't discount the possibility that he might be found not guilty," said Kim. "You know how clannish we are out here. Locals look out for one another. We don't have direct proof that he did anything; all we have is circumstantial. I'll give you a call when we know something. Okay?"

"I'd appreciate that, Kim," Dave said as the jeep stopped at his lodging.

After picking up his jeep the next day, Dave filed papers on the case. He still wondered whether the Crown had strong enough evidence. If Jack confessed, the case would be clean and over quickly. He hoped the Crown would reduce the charges to lesser ones, such as simple negligence. No, he thought, they wouldn't do that. Locals, as Kim said, might look out for one another, but opinions at Bob and Helen's café and other community gathering places were divided.

Dave left his office to find Kim. When he arrived at her station, she was rereading her notes from the night before.

"What do you think of the bear?" she asked when he came in. "Was it behind the shed or inside?"

"I thought inside," said Dave. "We ought to check out the place one more time before Jack makes bail and goes back there. We can check out his truck and skiff."

As they pulled up to Jack's house, Dave began to sweat, recalling his close call with the bear. Kim started her inspection of the house, making notes on a clipboard.

Inside the shed, Dave inspected the walls. Under a fresh coat of paint were claw marks, obviously made by a bear. On the ground were the indentation and molt of a bear. Scat clumps littered the room as well. The presence of the animal—added to the body parts fed to the bears, plus the flesh-filled garlic-and-pepper balls—pointed to Jack's involvement in the Gros Morne Park bear problem. But why? Norm Cotten, of course, had a financial motive for disposing of bodies. But Jack had been an outfitter leading hunters around the island killing bears. Why would he keep one around his property, knowing how dangerous and unpredictable the critters were? It just didn't add up.

"Jack's prepared for a long trip," said Kim. "I peeked into his vehicle."

"He can't leave the island," Dave said. "But if he gets bail, he may be free to go anywhere on it."

"Sure could," Kim agreed.

Looking through Jack's truck, Dave did not find anything directly linking Jack to the case of tampering with human remains.

"We may not have a case," he said.

"It happens more often than not," Kim replied. "But it would be good to see where all this leads."

Dave admired Kim's meticulous notes, neat and copious as though she were a scientist. At the very minimum, she would gather enough evidence to make a convincing case that Jack had violated several park and provincial laws, including feeding and domiciling a wild bear without a permit. The Criminal Code charge would address the tampering of bodies without a licence for medical or public health reasons. The laws against ghouls were long-standing in common law, dating from the centuries of body-snatching for witchcraft and private medical research. Cutting up human body parts for personal use was against the law, as was domesticating bears without a licence. But there the case against Jack stopped.

Officials had found doughnuts, pork and beef scraps inside the bears they had cropped in the park. The animals could just as easily have been feeding on garbage. Looking at the indentation in the ground where Jack's bear slept, Dave began to wonder about something else—the mysterious heart attacks of Mark Hughes, Dorothy Crandall and Rick Preston, and the coincidence of Norm Cotten's bear attack. In his semi-conscious state after the bear had knocked him down, he recalled the bear licking his face and clothes. Not typical in a bear attack.

Bears were ferocious predators. They seldom toyed with their victims; they killed rapidly, seizing the prey by the neck, breaking the spinal cord, or ripping off a limb and causing death by bleeding. A serious bear attack was never a pretty sight; the bear attack when he first arrived in the park demonstrated that. He and Kim had nearly been killed by what appeared to be a sow with her cub.

This time, however, the bear that attacked him seemed to be acting more like a trained police dog; it seemed to want to overpower him, not to kill him, at least not in the way bears would ordinarily kill someone.

When Kim entered the shed, she uncovered more information on the bear. It had been living there for some time. The tree bark around the fields had bear writing, one of the maples serving as the bear's sentinel post. As an outfitter, Jack had to know about the bear's presence. It was obviously partially domesticated, and it was Jack's, so he had been hiding it.

"I'll check around the crematorium again," she said. "Funny how Norm was attacked by a bear. Perhaps he was in the act of carrying body parts to his car when the bear got to him. And Jack found him. Coincidence?"

"It does seem suspicious in light of what we have found here," said Dave. "The bear that attacked me last night was not trying to kill me. It didn't bite me. It hit me. It was licking me while holding me down, and preventing me from rising and getting away. I think Jack was controlling it."

"So you were the bear's teddy bear, its rag doll," said Kim.

"No, I was Jack's toy. I could have been killed if he had wanted it to kill me."

"It's an interesting theory," said Kim, "but I don't think the judge will buy it. We would have a hell of a time proving something as complicated as that."

"It's not so far-fetched," said Dave. "Did you know that bears were trained in ancient times to kill people, sometimes slowly, *à la* cat and mouse? The victim died from exhaustion or fright. Either would trigger cardiac arrest."

"Really, Dave," said Kim, "A judge would laugh us out of court for charging him with training bears to frighten people to death, as though anyone wouldn't be frightened of a wild bear anyway."

"Don't you think it's odd? I mean, first the gravedigger, then Jack's wife, then Rick Preston, Norm and me. I was attacked by a bear but not killed by it …"

"Mrs. Crandall had already suffered a stroke," said Kim. "She could have easily died of fright. Jack seemed very fond of her. He had no reason to kill her."

"Preston was reckless," she added. "Norm fed bears human flesh all the time, which is always risking a bear attack. Every bear behaves differently. Some of them do toy with us, and maybe a few would play us to death. Jack isn't the bear. We don't have the bear as evidence, and nobody has reported seeing him with one. I dunno."

Dave began to realize that his theory, as plausible as it seemed to him, looked weak when he tried to explain it. At first, Jack had had his own little meat shop at the crematorium for feeding his own bear, it could be argued. That would have been an opportunity, initially. When things began to get out of hand in the park, he had to stop the bears from developing a taste for the flesh Norm had been feeding them.

"We always know more than we actually file in court," said Kim. "Maybe Jack did do what you're suggesting. We don't need it to get him for dismembering the bodies from the morgue."

18

Flight Risk

The next day, the story of Jack's arrest was front page news in *The Northern Examiner*, *The Western Gazette* and other media. It was news in all of Canada, and indeed, all of North America. BODY SNATCHER CAUGHT: LOCAL OUTFITTER, read the *Examiner* headline.

Bob's Big Stop Café, of course, was, as ever, news central, the root of the town's grapevine.

"I could smell the stink of flesh on his clothes," said a regular.

"He did it all at night," said Arthur, "under cover of darkness. Jack was a busy man. He and Norm must have been working together."

"I wonder who'll defend him in court," said Helen. "He'll need a good lawyer."

"Did you read how they figured out he was the one?" Arthur asked. "He was feeding the bears flesh with garlic and pepper in it. He must have been trying to cover his tracks. He was afraid that he had gone too far."

"Poor Dorothy," said Helen. "I'm glad she will never know about this."

Bob joined the conversation. "He'll have nothing after his legal bills."

So it went. The customers were divided, however; there were two camps. One thought that Jack ought to simply be fined. The other, consisting of clients of the funeral home, were furious and wanted Jack to suffer unspeakable, cruel punishment. Of those who were in neither camp, a tiny handful in the café consisting of Helen, Bob and a couple of old friends of Jack's, just wanted to wait and see what the decision would be in court.

What's the latest word on Jack? These words rang throughout Deer Lake.

The latest word was not long in coming. Jack could not post bail and would remain in prison until his trial, which would commence in a week. Dave also learned from Kim that Jack had rehired a lawyer named Nancy Cooper. That news cheered Kim, oddly, for it should not have, after the Crown's last encounter with Jack. Her sympathy for the outfitter was not uncommon around town. The island always seemed to have a wellspring of sympathy for outlaws, nonconformists and rugged individuals, even ones as odd and slightly nuts as Jack seemed to be.

Meanwhile, at the jail, Jack met with his defence attorney.

"Hello, Jack," said Nancy. "I haven't heard from you since last year. What can you tell me?"

They were talking in a small room at the Deer Lake jail reserved for attorneys.

"Well," he said, "I'm charged with body-snatching, body dismemberment and feeding the flesh of corpses to bears."

"Do you know the evidence against you?"

"Not really," he said. "They haven't told me much."

"Don't say any more to them," Nancy said.

The first order of business, she advised, was to tell her everything. Nancy led with questions and Jack answered.

"Okay," she said after a while. "This doesn't sound good."

"Can you tell me what my chances are?"

"Jack," she said, "mutilation and dismemberment of human corpses are not easily dismissed."

"What the hell," he said. "I know that already."

"You don't know the judge."

"I will."

Nancy told Jack she wanted to know more about his work and his relationship with Norm.

"I need you to be truthful with me," she said.

"I will be truthful."

Jack described to her all the gory details. In the time he had worked at the funeral home, he never suspected that Norm Cotten was feeding flesh to bears.

"On paper, his cremation billings were almost five times higher than the number I was actually cremating. No funeral home on this side of the island could match him."

"Do you have proof of Norm's feeding the bears flesh from his morgue?"

"No," said Jack. But then he recalled the body parts and Norm's admission to Jack. When he described the containers of human organs he had found in Norm's office, she almost fell off her chair. Her face turned green as waves of nausea hit her. He described how he had used human flesh to distribute the garlic-and-pepper deterrent.

"And what would make you think of doing that, Jack?"

"Norm had primed them to acquire a taste for people. I knew that some things would turn bears off certain foods they liked. I discovered that garlic and pepper would work if I could conceal the smell until the bears had ingested the food."

"And that was your only motive?"

"Yes."

Nancy sat back in her chair, trying to absorb and make sense of the implications. "Have the police told you anything?"

"Nothing of importance."

"They're telling me that you were deeply in debt."

"Sure thing, Ms. Cooper. They got that right. But it wasn't a secret."

"So we can verify that you weren't getting paid from Norm's thefts."

"That's easy enough to prove. What are my chances of going free?" he asked. "I don't want to put up a lot of money for a lost cause."

"Jack, this is very serious," she said. "Mutilation of corpses is not quite murder, but it's desecration of another person, even if that person is no longer alive. It's a kind of assault, like knowingly driving over someone already dead lying on the highway. You aren't guilty of killing the person, but you're guilty of assault. It's somewhere in between assault with intent to kill and simple assault, plus the desecration of the person and offence to relatives. It's serious enough to defend yourself as well as you can.

"Now," she continued, "about the garlic-and-pepper deterrent. That will be mitigating, but you still violated the law in acting that way."

"Yes."

"Did you do it to kill people?"

"No, I did not!"

"Well, thank the Lord for that," Nancy said. "Now, again, did you bait the bears with human flesh, Jack?"

"Yes."

"Why would you do such a thing?"

"To save people," he answered.

"What do you mean, save people? How can you save people by feeding the bears human flesh?"

"I ground up the flesh and fed the bears for a week or two, placing it in remote areas where I knew they'd easily discover it. After eating the bait laced with garlic and pepper, they'd become ill and be turned off eating that kind of food. They don't eat anything else for a day or two, because they get really severe heartburn. It's so strong that they could only drink water."

"I've known you from school, Jack," Nancy said. "And I know you wouldn't hurt anyone, not on purpose. How did you learn about this?"

"Baiting animals is a common poaching and sometimes conservation tactic that's been used for years. Go ahead and ask Kim Hollings."

"Kim at the ranger station?"

"That's her."

"So you thought you might be able to save people?"

"Yes."

"Do you think you have stopped the bear attacks around here?"

"Yes. It stopped over a month ago."

Nancy jumped up and ran around the table.

"You're a hero, Jack, not a murderer!" she exclaimed. "And I'm going to prove it. Just wait till I tell the media this story. Why, you'll be famous for saving Newfoundland when I'm finished, just wait and see! Now let's see if we can get you out of here. Let's go tell these good gentlemen your story."

Nancy, dressed in her court robe, made her plea before the magistrate. "Jack will plead guilty, Your Honour, to dismembering the bodies, but not for personal use. He'll plead not guilty to reckless disregard for public safety, he'll plead not guilty to violating the interests of the deceased and families of the deceased, and he'll plead not guilty to the charge of feeding the bears in the park."

The magistrate replied that the charges would nonetheless stand and the case would have to go to trial.

"We request bail, Your Honour," said Nancy.

"No, ma'am," the magistrate said. "Your client is to be arraigned Wednesday morning."

"It's only for two nights," she whispered in Jack's ear. "I think it would be in your best interest not to fight it. You can have visitors."

"I can't see that being a problem," he said. "Who besides you will be calling on me?"

"I'll see you a lot," Nancy said. "We have much work to do in a very short time. I'll devote all my time to the trial in the next two days. I can guarantee you that much, Jack."

When Nancy met with him the next day, she tried to explain the charges against him and why she didn't think a conviction was likely.

"These charges are dicey."

"I was trying to save people," Jack said.

"I know," said Nancy. "I'm sure no one will question your motive, though they may ask some things about your mental health. I mean, grave digging and cremations aren't the kind of career choices that come to mind for mentally healthy individuals. We face an image problem. Add the ghoulish behaviour, and you see the jury looking at someone they'll regard as a Frankenstein. I'm really sorry to put you through this. But I have to ask you, Jack, is there anything else you haven't told me?"

"Yes," he said. "I was done with it in August."

"You're a hero," she said. "You may become a legend here on the island some day when we're done with this trial."

Looking at Jack, in his orange prison suit, the lawyer wondered about her client, the teen she had known in high school. He had been a handsome fellow, popular but not studious, a jokester and something of a flirt. He would never have flirted with someone who looked as mousy as she had, with her thick glasses, hand-me-down clothes and acne. She was also overweight in high school, a contrast to her svelte figure now. She admired his independence and that he knew more about animals than anyone else. He was no angel, but she was convinced there was nothing macabre, sinister or fiendish about him. He was simply a guy with good motives who had applied himself illegally. Happens all the time.

It was clear in listening to Jack that he wouldn't hurt anyone unless he was defending himself or some other potential victim from harm. She thought that his taking the stand would work out; his testimony could win over the judge. Given the public outcry by the victimized families of the deceased, a trial by jury was too risky.

"How do you feel about me representing you?" she asked.

"I guess I know my women ... and women lawyers," Jack said. "I've got the best one on the island."

Nancy worked with her client from early that morning until four o'clock in the afternoon, preparing his testimony and testing him with prosecution-style questions.

"I wouldn't mind having some pizza," Jack said. "If you can join me for a couple of pieces."

"No," Nancy said. "I have to work. The gossips know more about your case than I do."

Hours later, she went outside the jail, the area near the gate was filled with reporters. The satellite transmission trucks and cars lining the street from the jail overflowed the parking lot. There were dozens of TV cameras. It looked like they had flown in from everywhere.

By eight o'clock that evening, there were over a thousand people blocking the streets. Reporters were camped out at the ranger station, Dave's headquarters and Norm's funeral parlour. They were stopping at every store in Deer Lake asking questions. Do you know Jack Crandall? What is he like? Does he strike you as being a murderer? Then there were reporters asking, "Would you give your body to save the Newfoundland people from bear attacks?"

At the airport, there was no more room for private planes to land and stay. People were carrying signs that read LET HIM GO, OUR BODIES ARE YOURS, HE'S SAVED US ALL and HE'S OUR HERO.

Nancy made a call to the Crown prosecutor; she wanted better control of the traffic and the crowds. By the next morning, there were no vehicles in that vicinity of town. Tents were set up on people's lawns and everyone opened their homes to anyone needing to use their washrooms.

That Wednesday morning there were two thousand people walking the streets of Deer Lake. When it was time for court, even the judge had to walk to the courthouse. Nancy, surrounded by police, had to walk four blocks to get there.

The courtroom was full of reporters. The judge had subpoenaed Dave and Kim and had given them questions to answer before the trial started. Now, after the court was called to order, he read the charges.

Nancy sat next to Jack. She leaned over and whispered, "What did I tell you? The Crown's taking all this very seriously. They're throwing the book at you, but don't worry."

"Thank you, Nancy," said Jack, shaking her hand. "You're a very smart lady."

The courtroom had quieted, except for the judge reading the charges, but the noise from demonstrators outside on the streets, both in support of and against Jack, was deafening. The judge apologized for the demonstrations held in front of the court.

"Maybe I can make it easier for everyone," the judge said. "What I'm about to do is not normal in a court of law, but this is not a normal case. I have read the testimonies of Dave Bishop, Newfoundland's chief biologist, and Ranger Kim Hollings, as well as the report from the RCMP. Would you four please come to the front of the courtroom?"

They walked to the front of the judge and the clerk administered the oaths.

The court clerk addressed the officials standing before him. "Do you Dave Bishop, Ranger Hollings, Captain Hann and Sergeant Cook, swear that your testimonies are the truth, the whole truth and nothing but the truth, so help you God?"

"Yes,," each replied.

"Thank you. Please be seated."

The judge beckoned to Jack to come forward. "Jack Crandall, please stand before the court."

Jack rose from his seat, and in front of the bench, he was sworn in by the court clerk.

"The written statement you have given this court is the truth, Mr. Crandall?"

"Yes, Your Honour, it is."

"Well," the judge said. "Let me make it very clear to you and everyone else present that what you have done is wrong."

Angry murmuring broke out in the room. The judge swung his gavel. "Silence! I want silence in this court!"

"Thank you," said the judge when order had been re-established.

"Let me say again, Mr. Crandall," he continued, "what you have done is wrong, very wrong. However, you have single-handedly saved dozens of people from death. Already a group has established a toll-free number to call and register organ donations. Jack Crandall, you have pleaded guilty to dismembering a human corpse, but not for personal use, is that correct?"

"Yes, Your Honour, that is correct."

"Then I have no choice but to find you guilty." There were protests from the spectators. Again the judge hit the wooden base with his gavel to silence the court.

"Thank you," he said when order was again restored.

"On this charge," the judge continued, "you are sentenced to two years less a day and fined five thousand dollars."

Nancy immediately jumped up and stood before the judge. "We will appeal," she said.

"Duly noted," said the judge. "On the second charge, Jack Crandall, of causing the death to visitors and residents of Newfoundland, I have found no evidence of this in the testimonies given to me by the witnesses. Therefore I am dropping the charge."

The prosecutor this time stood up and protested. "But Your Honour, you can't do this!"

"Willard, you are not going to get famous over this case, so sit down! That is my decision," the judge replied. "You may appeal it, too."

Voices and murmurs rose once again, and again the judge silenced the outcries.

"Your Honour," asked Nancy, "my client requests bail pending his appeal of the sentence."

"I object," the prosecutor said. "Mr. Crandall is a flight risk."

The judge shuffled through a few papers on the bench. He beckoned the accused to the front of the court again. The prosecutor and Nancy stood on either side of Jack.

"Normally," the judge said, "I would heed the opposition to bail on a charge of this magnitude pending appeal of judgment. But I see Mr. Crandall had a previous charge, the terms of which he has fulfilled. There is an affidavit from park biologist Dave Bishop recommending clemency for the defendant, stating that the defendant saved his life from a bear attack. Mr. Bishop also explained that the crime, mutilation of the corpses intended for cremation at the funeral home, was an act undertaken to prevent bears from attacking people for food. It was an act of desperation, instigated out of an exigency that authorities failed to address clearly. I am not sure whether Mr. Crandall's appeal will succeed. But I am also not sure whether he is guilty of the charges, as I understand them, beyond the statutory violations. Therefore, I am granting him bail. So ruled, this matter is no longer before us."

Jack turned to his counsel. "Thank you, Nancy."

"Give me a call," she said, collecting her things.

Dave and Kim watched as court officers led Jack away to be processed before releasing him.

Epilogue

A Man and a Bear

Early the next day, Dave woke up and made coffee. He was thinking about the trial and the misfit, Jack Crandall. Kim had told him about Jack's background, including his connection with Rick Preston and Rick's role in the death of Jack's son. There was much more to Jack's story that was equally intriguing. As a young widow, Jack's mother had remarried. Jack was a young boy, Kim said, and had been raised in a small town out east. Jack's adoptive father was charged with child abuse. He was convicted and Jack and his mother moved to Corner Brook, where he graduated from high school, met his wife and married.

Now Dave understood why Jack hadn't seemed depressed and distraught over the loss of his loved ones. His grief had been transformed into anger as a result of his abusive upbringing.

It was curious, Dave thought, that a number of reported cases of child abuse mentioned the social isolation of the victims. Many of the children wound up as misfits, outcasts and loners, trying to escape social situations. Some no doubt found the company of animals and the outdoors less threatening to their equilibrium. It was understandable. But Dave also guessed that there would be a great deal of rage in such a person—a silent, hidden rage that exploded out of nowhere, violent and deadly, much like a black bear that ambushes its victims. He wondered how Jack would make out on appeal and considered writing another letter on his behalf, for a commuted or reduced sentence.

For now there was no more for him to do. He lay down again and closed his eyes. For the first time in several weeks he dozed off in a wink. The morning quickly passed into noon.

In the afternoon when the tide rose, fluffy white clouds from the Gulf of St. Lawrence blew over the park. Gusts of wind lifted up columns of leaves covering the forest floor. The ocean tide rose, the waves slapped rhythmically against the large flat rocks shielding the shore and the breakers roared. On the shore road, a truck had collided into a pine tree. The front end was smashed into the tree trunk. The door on the driver's side was flung open, the windshield smashed, and the front hood twisted. But there was no driver.

The only sign of life was a large kingfisher circling close to the truck, ready to pounce on any small prey. Hovering in the distance were smaller scavenger birds. When it found no food, the kingfisher made its exit, leaving the truck to seagulls and crows. The birds squawked and jumped about the cab and rear pan looking for scraps. They picked at clumps of bear scat at the scene and they inspected bear paw prints near the truck that led into the forest.

In an hour there was only the sound of the ocean resting at full tide. And when night fell there was still the truck smashed into the tree.

Kim received word of the accident. The police informed her there were signs of a bear involved in a possible missing-persons report.

"The truck was on a road going north along the coast," he said.

It was Jack's truck.

Kim's first reaction was to call Dave to let him know. She also telephoned Nancy Cooper, Jack's attorney, to find out what she knew of Jack's whereabouts. Cooper, of course, didn't have a clue. Later in the day, Kim accompanied the police as they searched Jack's property, but nothing there looked suspicious. All indications were that he had planned to return to the house. His packed skiff was on the trailer and his other possessions boxed and ready for travel. The blood in and around the truck was identified as belonging to Jack, so the police obtained a court order to seize and secure his property, pending an investigation into his disappearance.

The buzz at the Big Stop Café contended that Jack had staged the accident and intended to hide in the back country. If so, they figured he had a fifty-fifty chance of survival in the north.

"I think he's dead," said Betty. "Poetic justice if he was killed and eaten by a bear, probably one of those he had fed somebody else to. Serves him right."

The discussions on the street fuelled speculation about the case. For weeks, local oddsmakers in Corner Brook were taking bets that Jack would be declared dead and his case closed. That bet soon proved to be a bad one.

A motion filed in court by Nancy Cooper asked the judge in the case to rule that Jack be declared dead. The Crown objected, stating it was premature to declare Jack Crandell deceased. The prosecution's argument won out, and Jack was ruled a fugitive from justice.

Life went on in Gros Morne National Park; the seasons changed, and a new year began with rumours of sightings of a man with an animal as a companion. In late March, a trapper reported seeing a black bear with a man who looked like Jack Crandall. He had observed the two figures on the opposite side of the Humber River. The bear was very large, the trapper said, a critter too big to view any closer than through a scope. It had a bright white star marking on its chest. The man and bear had been in view for only a few seconds before they disappeared into the brush.

Later that spring, a logger near the park reported seeing a man on a path around a remote lake. Through his high-powered binoculars, the logger saw that the man was haggard-looking and dressed like a woodsman, carrying what appeared to be a fishing rod. The logger was startled to see a large black bear trundling close beside the man, at times running ahead like a playful puppy. When the stranger stopped to fish, the bear stopped also.

The man fished away and fed his catch to the bear. As the fisherman sat on a log, the animal licked the side of his face, and, astonishingly, laid its large head on the man's lap as if it were a house pet, allowing the man to wrap an arm around its head and hug it. When the two disappeared into the woods, the logger rode his four-wheeler to the scene. However, he could not find any tracks of the man or of the bear, only patches of late snow on the trail. There were no signs of life, except for a couple of Canadian jays flitting about overhead.

Reports of Jack sightings grew in number and detail. A popular story in circulation was that of Jack and the bear supposedly dancing around a fresh moose carcass. Still another hunter circulated an account of a man playing a fiddle as a bear pranced around a campfire. After a few weeks, it was hard to tell whether reports of Jack and the bear were true or simply rumours in Gros Morne park and Deer Lake.

During the tourist season, there were never any confirmed reports of Jack, yet hikers from the far corners of the globe would follow the marked paths through the pine trees and around gorges and ravines, in search of the elusive Jack Crandall and his bear, Starlight.

Panting and climbing, they trekked in search of the legend of Gros Morne park. They would push through the alder, duck under fallen pines, and in their eagerness, noisily crunch the twigs and dried leaves on the forest floor. They would climb up the slippery granite sides of the mountains nearly touching white billowy clouds above.

In and around Gros Morne, all through the summer, hikers, adventurers and campers brought fresh rumours when they descended from the mountains.

Some reported that "Jack" hung meat from trees, buried stores of vegetables and set strange snares and traps for rabbits and other small game. Farmers around the park reported crops stolen and farm chickens and eggs missing. Soon, the petty thefts prompted them to boast, "Jack and the bear called." The incidents were too trifling to be of much concern to the authorities, since there were no signs of the culprit aside from bear tracks. The tracks, however, gave life to the surmise that Jack had an accomplice. There were obvious forgeries, handwritten notes left at some of the break-ins stating the gratitude of the thief, in script proven not to belong to Jack, stating, "Thank you. Jack and bear."

The jokes were at the victim's expense, with the reporter in question usually emanating a powerful smell of the island rum, SCREECH.

While there has never been proof of a crime committed by Jack and the bear, "robbed by a man and a bear" quickly became another island myth.

Although none of the victims, nor anyone else, have ever photographed the elusive fugitive, Newfoundland's Gros Morne

National Park is full of bears with white stars on their chests, walking on the tops of wind-stunted pine trees. A sad few may see one of them dashing from view under the tuckamore. Be well advised not to pursue the bear, for the path that it has taken leads only to the spot where it will ambush those who would hunt it down.

Sign in Gros Morne National Park:
PLEASE DO NOT FEED THE BEARS

Bear Facts and Safety

Bear Facts

The North American Black Bear, *Ursus americanus*, is normally black with a brownish muzzle and often has a white star-shaped patch on its chest. Its coat may also have variations of black and brown, beige, cinnamon, and occasionally white.

The black bear is an omnivorous scavenger. The bulk of its diet consists of vegetation; however, it will also eat insects, fish, small mammals, and carrion. Clocked at short-burst speeds of over thirty miles per hour, the black bear will often hunt and run down young deer, elk, caribou and moose for food. A bear is hungry most of the time, going without foraging for no more than an hour, and will gorge itself to satiation when it eats flesh of any kind. A bear can eat forty-five to fifty pounds at one sitting, and, when it is not hibernating, a bear can add five pounds a day to its weight.

The black bear is a skilled hunter and is able to sense the location and approach of its prey. While it has relatively poor eyesight, the black bear has an extremely keen sense of smell and its hearing exceeds human frequency ranges. The black bear's nasal mucosa is about a hundred times larger than in humans; it will often stand on its hind legs with its nose in the air to detect any appealing scents. The black bear has an intuitive sense of how to ambush a prey, the bear's favourite tactic in hunting. It knows how to disguise its ambush trails, often backtracking from an attack point and sweeping the trail free of debris, brushes, twigs, leaves and loose pebbles that would give away the bear's location. Moreover, a bear is an excellent camouflage artist, having the ability to lower the perceptible indications of its vital signs, breathing, pulse, odour and movement, in order to mask its presence from many hunting dogs.

Bears generally excel as swimmers and are frequently seen crossing rivers and small lakes. They are also adept at climbing trees. Cubs will often take to trees when frightened.

General Precautions in Black Bear Territory

All wild animals, even domesticated animals usually found in the wild, are dangerous. Always be informed of the habits of wild animals when you are in the wilderness. You should consult with park managers and rangers in bear country to learn safety precautions before you camp or before you set out on your hike.

Most bears will try to avoid direct contact with humans. If you warn them of your presence, they will usually move out of the area. To avoid a bear encounter, you should travel in groups and make a lot of noise. Hike only in the daylight and try to stay in open areas. If you are hiking near running water, be conscious of the fact that the noise of the water may cover the sound of your approach. Also, if you are walking into the wind, a bear situated upwind of you will not smell your approach. Keep children close to you and dogs on a leash. A dog could anger a bear and lead it straight back to you! Bears will defend their food, so use caution when travelling near natural food sources. A female bear will also protect her cubs; never pass between the two!

If you do encounter a bear, keep calm and do not attempt to run away. Back away slowly, and talk in a soft voice. Do not turn around so that your back is to the bear; you want to keep an eye out for any sign of aggression. If the bear begins to swing its head from side to side, make sounds such as snorts, whoops, huffs or moans, display its teeth or claws, swat at the ground, pant, make eye contact or flatten its ears back, it is an indication that the bear is upset and you should give it more space.

There are two types of bear attacks. One is a defensive attack, which usually occurs if you surprise a bear and it trys to defend itself or its cubs. If contact cannot be avoided, you should play dead. Lie on your stomach with your legs apart and try to protect your face, neck and head with your arms. Keep quiet until the bear leaves.

An offensive attack occurs at night or when a bear has been stalking you and decides to attack. You should *not* play dead in an offensive attack, rather you should try to escape to a secure place. A vehicle would be ideal. Climb a tree if you must, but be aware that you cannot out-climb a black bear any more than you can outrun it.

Attempting to fight off a bear attack with sticks, rocks or anything you can use as a weapon may sometimes work to stop such an attack. Some people have reported that a sharp blow to the bear's nose, accompanied by waving their hands and shouting at it, has made it retreat from an attack. In the woods, however, it is wise to have an air horn or other noise device to frighten off an attacking bear. As a last resort, spraying it with bear spray may deter an imminent bite from a bear, but these sprays must be used with caution. Keep in mind that a two-year-old bear can easily overpower most people, even professional fighters and hunters.

Needless to say, even panhandling bears in camps are potential attackers. Food, garbage and perfumed items, along with dishes and containers of all types, will attract bears. These items should never be left unattended and should always be stored so that bears cannot get at them. Barbecue picnic areas, campgrounds, garbage dumps and outdoor toilets are sites that regularly attract bears. Use caution in all of these areas, especially in the evening and at night.

For general guidelines on bear safety tips, consult the following Web sites:

1. **www.advertisenorth.com**
2. **www.mountainnature.com/wildlife/bears**
3. **www.bear.org/Black/Black_Bear_Facts.html**
4. **www.bear.org/Kids/Black_Bear_Facts_Kids.html**

5. **www.bearbiology.com/bbdesc.html**
6. **www.hww.ca/hww2.asp?pid=1&id=83&cid=8**

and see the "You Are In Black Bear Country" pamphlet produced by Parks Canada.

For a general overview of bear attacks on people, *Bear Attacks: Their Causes and Avoidance* Revised Edition by Stephen Herrero (Lyons Press, 2002) is one of the most informative sources. *Bear Attacks*, first published in 1985, is the authoritative study of attacks on humans by the great grizzly and the occasionally deadly black bear. Herrero, a professor of Environmental Science and Biology at the University of Calgary, is recognized throughout the world as a leading authority on bear ecology, behaviour and attacks.

About the Author

Walter Mallery has been a hunting guide in Canada for over twenty-five years. Born in Sussex, New Brunswick in 1952, he was raised on a farm, where he learned woodcraft and hunting. He has been a woodsman for forty years, during which time he has hunted trophy bears, fished in salmon and trout tournaments, and travelled and hunted in both the United States and Canada.

In and around Sussex he is well known as an oral storyteller, a 4-H leader and a member of various organizations, including the Goshen Snowmobile Association, international hunting associations and local conservation groups. He is a certified master technician for Arctic Cat and the owner of Walt's Snowmobile Shop Ltd., Walt's Guiding and Outfitting, and a hunting and game lodge.

Walter Mallery lives in Springdale, New Brunswick with his wife, Betty, and Sadie, his hunting dog. He has one daughter and one granddaughter.